W9-ANP-572

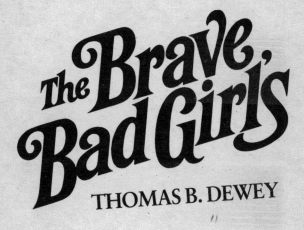

The Brave, Bad Girls

THOMAS B. DEWEY

Carroll & Graf Publishers, inc.

New York

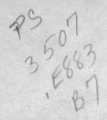

Published by arrangement with the author.

First Carroll & Graf edition 1985

Carroll & Graf Publishers, Inc.
260 Fifth Avenue
New York, NY 10001

ISBN: 0-88184-176-5

Manufactured in the United States of America

This book is for
Shirley Collier, Edith Brett and Sidney Satenstein

She was there, as she had said she would be. It was no trick to spot her. Her vague, breathless description by telephone half an hour earlier had not told me much, but she was the only lone woman in the place and she was watching the door.

It took some time for them to get me to her. The maitre d'hotel had to do some hemming and hawing, take care of a few other customers, dispatch a captain to check with her—all of which was normal enough: I was the wrong type of patron.

I stood now in the fun room of one of the few remaining traditional halls of ritz. You could get in all right, given the price, a fair skin, a relatively straight nose and a conservative manner. Even a "theatrical person," if prominent and employed, could get in.

The maitre d's job was eased by the fact that few off-beat types cared to get in. The room was high, wide and coldly furnished, with many lights. The dance floor was designed for conversational, rhythmic walking. Although the music was chiefly by Berlin, Cole Porter, Rodgers, Kern and Romberg, after the first half hour it all began to sound like Strauss.

The maitre d' finally cleared his throat at me and I followed him by a winding route to her table. It overlooked the dance floor from between two well-trimmed potted palms and it was covered by a white linen cloth.

On it now were two napkins, one discreetly rumpled and showing a stain of lipstick, two silver settings, an empty water goblet, a thin-stemmed cocktail glass half full of champagne and cognac, a small patent leather purse and a pair of carefully tanned, red-tipped, young female hands.

I said something to the maitre d' about a martini and he went away. I adjusted the chair to the seat of my pants and my tie around my neck, looked at the girl and said, "Hello, Miss Turner."

"Thank you for coming so quickly," she said.

I looked at her some more. She had brown eyes in a tanned, firmly rounded face and dark, lustrous hair, Italian cut. The red on her lips was subtly provocative. She was loaded with class. Also, she was awfully young. When the waiter brought my martini, I had the feeling that it was probably illegal, not only for her to be here, but for me to be with her.

Across the room, the orchestra, smooth and stringy, had finished a medley from *Showboat* and the musicians were parking their instruments for a break. She had turned her head and was watching them. I was still watching her. When she noticed it, she turned to me, smiling with those young, red lips.

"It's a shame really," she said. "The music's so dull —so routine, and all those talented boys——"

"I'm not much of a critic."

"But you know what you like."

I looked at her steadily.

"I can't tell yet," I said.

"I'm sorry," she said. "It was a very corny remark."

"What did you want me to do?"

"Do?"

"You said you were frightened."

"That's true."

She was watching the nearly deserted bandstand again. All the musicians had drifted away except for the pianist, who stood at the keyboard of a concert grand, sorting music. The rustle of conversation in the half-filled room was controlled and distant.

"I wanted you to take me home," she said.

I waited for her to look at me again. When she did, her eyes were wide and young and appealing. It may have been calculated, but it was extremely effective.

"You see," she said, "I really am frightened. I'm just trying not to be messy about it."

"Don't try too hard. I've been scared myself."

"That's hard to believe."

"At your age," I said, "I was scared quite often. Now I try to avoid frightening situations."

She frowned and took a drink.

"That has a special meaning, I think," I said. "Don't take it as a lecture from an 'older man.' "

Her face winced before the frown vanished. Then she was smiling across the table with sudden, girlish frankness.

"I think you're sweet," she said. "I guess I'm just being silly."

"I never meant to say you're not honestly frightened."

She picked up the shiny black purse and put one of her hands in it. The hand came out holding a couple of folded bills. She slid them across the table.

"Before I forget," she said.

The two bills totaled two hundred dollars. I refrained from picking them up.

"This is to pay me for taking you home?"

"Isn't it enough?" she said. "I don't have any more with me, except for a few——"

"Who's after you?"

She looked at me quickly and the girlish frankness went away. "I don't know exactly," she said. "I don't see that it makes much difference. If that isn't enough money——"

"I have to know what's going on."

She tucked her lower lip between her teeth and shook her pretty head vaguely.

"I don't understand. I thought——"

"You thought that all you had to do to hire a private detective was to hand him some money and say 'let's go'?"

Her eyes now were chilly and withdrawn.

"I'm not holding out for the detailed history of your life," I said. "If you're in trouble, if you have guilty knowledge, I don't want to know about it. None of my business. But if you want a protective escort, I have to know what I'm up against. I might want to call in some help."

She looked across the empty dance floor to where the musicians were slowly gathering.

"I see——" she said.

"That's what I meant about avoiding frightening situations. As far as the money is concerned, the police will protect you for nothing."

She sipped at her drink.

"If you like," I said, "I'll be glad to call the police for you and wait till they come."

She came around then, fast and definite.

"No, not the police. And I haven't—I mean I haven't *done* anything really——"

"All right. How much can you tell me?"

After about thirty seconds she leaned across the table and came out with it—or some of it.

"You have to believe I don't just go out by myself this way, looking for someone to pick up——"

"I believe it."

"I have a fiancé—he's in the army, so I don't date. But once in a while I go out alone, to a place like this, just to be around people for a change."

"Sure."

"I don't drive. I take a taxi. Tonight, when I left the apartment, there were two men hanging around outside."

"You ever see them before?"

She hesitated, then shook her head.

"No. I didn't pay much attention really. But after we'd got started, the taxi driver told me we were being followed. Naturally, I was worried."

"Did you check up on him, the taxi driver?"

She spread her hands.

"How could I? I don't know about these things. But after I'd got into the hotel, I tried to find out. Instead of coming right in here, I went to the desk in the lobby and asked the clerk about something—I forget what— and then I turned around, fast, you know?—and went to the door and looked out."

"And they were there?"

"Yes. I think it was the same two men. Maybe not. Maybe I'm just being silly——"

"You don't have any idea who they were?"

"No."

"There were just the two of them?"

"Yes."

"Do you live alone?"

"I have an apartment of my own, not far away."

I looked at her, then at the money on the table, then at her again, but now she was looking at the musicians. The music had struck a livelier tempo than before and I could hear her foot tapping faintly. I wondered what was so fascinating to her over there, considering her remark about the "dull, routine music."

The story she had told me was not the best in the world. Maybe it was all right for now and the best she could do, but I wished she hadn't brought out all that money in advance.

She turned, as if she had read my mind. Her voice was soft and quick.

"Please pick up the money. The waiter's coming."

I couldn't see what that had to do with it, but I picked up one of the bills, shaking the second one loose.

"Just half of it," I said.

She blinked those big brown eyes.

"But——"

"Suppose it should get around," I said, "that I had to have two whole bills, just to see a beautiful girl home?"

She blushed then becomingly, picked up the second

bill and stuffed it into her purse. The waiter waited respectfully.

"Check, please," I said.

He bowed and went away. Miss Turner finished her drink, dabbed at her lips with the napkin, picked up her purse and got on her feet. I got up too.

"If you'll excuse me," she said, "I'll be ready in a minute."

She walked away among the tables, young and alive and self-assured. I still didn't know how old she was—twenty-one maybe—or nineteen. But there was plenty of wonderful woman in her and it would keep getting better for many years to come.

The waiter had to go away to get change and when he came back, Miss Turner had not yet returned. I scooped up the change and with it a note, written on hotel stationery, short and to the point.

"Please meet me at the rear exit in about five minutes. Sherry Turner."

I gave the waiter half a buck and he seemed grateful.

"The rear exit," I said. "How do I get there?"

He showed me and went away.

2.

At the end of a narrow corridor, a red light glowed above the frosted glass pane of the single door. When I opened it and looked out, I found the service area of the hotel on my left—a big receiving entrance and a space beyond, along the concrete wall, for trash and garbage cans. On my right, a high wire fence enclosed the parking lot. Between the fence and the building, a wide, paved areaway extended fifty feet straight ahead. It ended at the alley that bisected the block, bordering the parking lot and continuing out of sight behind the rear wing of the hotel.

I let the door swing to and waited, leaning against the wall. I had the feeling you have with a mild fever —you recognize everyone, you know what you're doing, but at the same time, everything is oddly shaded. I couldn't find a reason for it. I just stood there feeling it, stuck with it, because I had some of her money in my pocket, along with definite instructions. Besides, she was pretty and very young.

She looked awfully good coming down the corridor in a floating walk, with that delicate, birdlike rhythm that I guess they learn in ballet. When she got to where I stood, she was slightly breathless, looking up at me out of those eyes.

"I'm sorry I made you wait," she said.

"It's all right. Only why do we leave by the rear?"

She seemed surprised.

"I thought you would want to," she said. "They were hanging around out in front. This way, we can go through the alley to the street and catch a taxi——"

"I have a car in the parking lot."

"Oh, I didn't know."

"All right," I said, "I can pick up the car later."

I pushed the door open and waited. She hesitated with her white teeth on her lip.

"If you'd rather go the other way——"

"No," I said. "That rest-home atmosphere depresses me."

She stepped out past me and we walked over the paved areaway toward the alley. Her feet in the flat ballet shoes made no sound.

Short of the corner of the building, she stopped and put her hand on my arm.

"Let's go back the other way," she said. "I'm afraid."

"We'll do whatever you say, but try not to be afraid."

She let go of my arm, stiffened a little in the shoulders and got started again. At the corner, I was on the inside near the wall and she went around wide, putting some space between us, as if to prove she wasn't scared after all. I smiled in the dark.

Then she had stopped again and turned back, running. She banged into me, grabbing my coat, and spoke in a hoarse whisper.

"Look out!"

I tried to see beyond her, but she pushed away and started to run and by the time I got focused on—as I had put it earlier—what I was up against, she was making good time down the alley toward the street, a long half-block ahead. The last I saw of her was a flash of white petticoat against the black, dirty wall of the apartment house behind the hotel.

There were two of them, as she had told me earlier. She hadn't bothered to tell me they were highly skilled meat handlers, but maybe she hadn't known this. Still, I remember thinking, I wonder why she didn't at least scream or something?

Naturally, I put up a fight. I hit the big one in front of me in the stomach and kicked the other one in the shin. But after that, the party was all theirs. The fact that there was no sense in the attack, that I had done nothing to bring it on, made it less bad than it might have been. It's when you have a chance to calculate it in advance that it hurts the most. You bring something extra to it.

Still, it hurts plenty. It hurts very badly at the beginning. After a while it levels off and you begin to go numb. Then when they quit, it starts really to hurt. You lie there where they dropped you. The alley pavement is cold, but you don't mind that. You would like it to be still and hard, instead of shifting and rolling under you, but you don't mind the cold. Your stomach is opening and closing like a poisonous flower, but you can't quite get it to give anything up. You are fully conscious and wish you weren't and you can't see much of anything, but you can hear very well indeed, even over the steady buzzing deep inside your head.

". . . get the car . . ."

. . . the sound of footsteps, receding, then the faint swish of traffic, a horn honking, and in your ear against the cold cement, the small, restless sounds that must be vibrations but which might also be the scurrying footsteps of rats running.

Time is without meaning. The car is there long before it could really have been brought up. You hear the engine. A door is opened. They lay hands on you again in a different way and for a moment you hang suspended by legs and shoulders. You hear them grunting with the strain, a couple of grumbled curses, and then you fall once more and it's as if everything inside you were broken and all the broken parts had razor edges.

You lie on the floor of the back seat, crowded by the big feet of the man riding with you. The motion of the car is worse than the heaving cement of the alley. You hurt too much to be angry and you're conditioned not to cry, so you take it out on your jaws and teeth. After a while you realize this and relax the muscles and get your teeth open. By now your stomach has managed to get to work and you let it happen, trying to keep it quiet, hoping it won't smell too much, because it might make him sore and you'd entertain one of those big feet in the lower back. Finally, happily, letting go with a rush, like descending in a runaway elevator, you pass out.

3.

Unhappily, I came to. The car windows were open and cold air swirled over me. I saw no bright lights and guessed we were in the remote suburbs. I was in no condition to take much interest. I could feel anger again, though, and that was a good sign. I dreamed up a few suitable tortures to be applied to them, either separately or as a team. At the moment, it was the best I could do. I didn't even know who they were.

The car slowed suddenly, twisted and climbed a low ramp, then rolled on slowly for some distance and stopped. The engine died. The door opened beyond my head and the big feet prodded at me.

"Out," a voice said.

I rolled over and got on my hands and knees. It was quite a sensation. I looked through the open door and one of them was standing out there, waiting for me. He couldn't seem to stand still. Or maybe there were several of him, like wax figures on a slowly revolving turntable.

I crawled through the door into the fresh air, missed the step and fell into him. He grabbed me soon enough and held me on my feet while the other one came out. By then the earth had settled some, I was less dizzy and I found I could walk, but there was little pleasure in it.

We stood at the rear of a high, ivy-covered English mansion, maybe in Glencoe or Winnetka. The grounds and the drive over which we had come were dark, but there were lights inside the house. Farther to the rear, beyond the three-car garage in front of which we had stopped, was a smaller building, a miniature of the house, also lighted inside. A winding stone path led to it from the drive. That was the route we took, the three of us, with me in the middle.

The big one was real big. The other was my height, but heavier. Once in a while, when some bruised nerve in my belly or chest sent off a new urgent message, I would lose my balance and fall against one or the other of them.

The little house turned out to be a detached study, or den. The big one handled a brass knocker on a recessed door and we waited. When I reached out to brace myself against the door, the big one knocked my hand down. I tried to look at him, to plant his face in my memory, but it was dark.

The door opened and a man peered out at us, then backed off inside, saying, "Bring him in."

Somehow they brought me in over the doorstep. I stood blinking in a dimly lighted, paneled study with bookshelves hung on the walls and an oversized mahogany desk. There were some chairs of different types and they all looked good. I stood there.

The one who had opened the door was peering at me. I decided he was nearsighted. He wore a smoking jacket and there was a book under his arm. He was around sixty years old. He had one of those stiff, handsome faces that gives you the idea that if you hit it with a hard rock, you would draw sparks instead of blood. His hair was white and the smoking jacket was in faultless taste. There was no odor of tobacco about him.

The two sluggers were hanging around in the vicinity and the guy got his eyes off me for a minute and spoke in a voice with starch in it.

"This isn't Kadek!"

One of them shuffled his feet. "He was with her at the hotel," he said. "They came out together. We figured ——"

"Who is he?"

There was some hesitation. Finally the smaller one said, "I don't know. He was with her. It was dark——"

Starchy was staring at me again. "What's your name?" he said.

The hell with that. I turned away, found a chair and

sank into it. The leather upholstery was cool and comforting. I relaxed against it and closed my eyes, hearing the sound of various pairs of feet.

"There's a way to find out," one of them said.

I let him find my wallet. There was a guarded gentleness in the way he went about it. I opened my eyes and looked at him as he backed away. It wasn't a bad face: not handsome, but neither ugly; not young, not old. It was impassive but not dead. It could have belonged to another private eye; or to an accountant, except that it had been outdoors too much. Maybe a used-car salesman.

The white-haired man held out his hand and the salesman gave him the wallet. He wasn't too nosy. He flipped it open, but all he looked at was the ID card under the plastic window. He took a short look, then a longer one. Then he groaned and handed the wallet to me.

"Oh, God," he said tiredly. "You know who he is?"

He told them. One of them whistled softly. I put the wallet back in my pocket.

"Well," one of them started, "how would we know?"

"Shut up," the man in the smoking jacket said.

He went to his desk, put down his book and opened a drawer. He came up with a full bottle of brandy and a small glass. He filled the glass and brought it to me. I drank it, dribbling a little. It felt good.

"Give him a cigaret," he said to them.

"What good would that do?" I said. "I can't breathe much as it is."

"I'm sorry," he said and went back to his desk.

"What happened to Sherry?" he asked.

One of them cleared his throat. "She ran off."

He sat there behind the big desk and drummed on it with long fingers. He looked as if he had a way to handle most things, but he wasn't sure about this. When he finally made up his mind, it seemed natural enough. He opened another drawer and brought out a check-book. I watched him make it out, firmly, not hesitating, not pausing to reckon an amount. He tore it out of the book, came around the desk and handed it to me.

It was for five hundred dollars, made out to "Cash" and signed "Roscoe Turner." Roscoe—Sherry. Father and daughter? brother and sister? uncle and niece? husband and wife? I wasn't curious enough to stay with it.

I crumpled the check in my stiff fingers, made a wad of it and tossed it back to him. It fell on the floor and he left it there.

"Oh, come now——" he said.

"Oh, come now?" I looked up at him. "That the way these things are handled? A quick settlement—everything okay—forget it?"

He didn't like it very well, but he didn't make any fuss. "If you'd rather take it to court," he said.

He was safe enough in that and he must have known it. I tried to get out of the chair but couldn't. The two meat handlers stepped in and helped me—gently. When I got up my eyes were on a level with Turner's.

"Who's Kadek?" I asked.

He just shook his head.

"It's nothing to me," I said. "I thought somebody ought to warn him."

He looked at the big one on my right. "Take him

home. If he wants a doctor, call one. I'll take care of the fee."

I made my way to the door, the two of them flanking me. The smaller one, the salesman, opened the door. Turner had come along behind us. He reached up as if to pat my shoulder, then either couldn't go through with it or was afraid of hurting me. He opened his mouth to say something and I beat him to it, using two old English words of four and three letters each, respectively. He didn't seem surprised.

"I regret that it happened," he said. "If you need anything, my business telephone is listed."

I looked at his starched face. "Oh," I said, "I thought you were going to say 'no hard feelings.'"

"Good night," he said.

He turned back to his desk. I and my two companions went out in the fresh air and climbed into the car. They gave me the back seat all to myself.

I was only half-conscious when they pulled up in front of my office-apartment on the Near North Side. But after they'd helped me out and I'd got a whiff of air and recognized my own surroundings, I braced up. They started up the stone steps with me, but I pulled away, got hold of the iron railing and looked at them where they stood.

"We were never really introduced," I said.

They looked at each other and the salesman cleared his throat. "We're in the security business," he said.

"For the government?"

No answer.

"For Turner?"

Still no answer.

"You want us to get a doctor?" he said.

"No. Suppose I wanted to look you up some day?"

The smaller one shook his head at me. "I wouldn't bother," he said. "Sorry about the misunderstanding, but you better try to forget it."

"Or?" I said.

He shrugged and they started down the steps. From the sidewalk he looked back at me. "You do business on a license, don't you?"

"That's right."

"Well, hang onto it, Mac. Don't lose it."

They crossed to the car, got in and drove away. The full meaning of his threat didn't come through to me until after I had got my clothes off, taken a couple of codeine pills with a glass of milk and crawled painfully into bed. I tried to stay awake to think it over, but the codeine worked fast and I didn't get far with it.

4.

I stayed in bed for a couple of days. A G.P. in the neighborhood came over and taped up my chest. He replenished my drug supply and I spent a lot of time sleeping. I'm not much of a masochist.

In the middle of the first day I made it into the office, called the hotel and arranged for them to send my car home. It took a little time and, when the guy got there with it, considerable money.

Aside from that, it was a restful routine. When I got hungry—and when my stomach would hold it— I would call Tony's joint across the street and he would send something over by one of the waitresses. They were good, hardworking girls and each in her own way expressed suitable regrets at my condition. They were my only visitors. The telephone rang once in a while, but each time it was nothing.

By noon on the third day, Monday, I felt up to collecting my mail from the floor under the slot in the door. Except for one item, it was no more than the telephone calls. The exception was an envelope from a firm called "American Electronics, Inc.," with an address in South Chicago. Inside was a check signed by Roscoe Turner. The price had advanced. This one was for a thousand dollars.

I wondered why he was so nervous. There was nothing I could do to him. An ordinary, peaceable citizen might get judgment in a court for unprovoked assault. But with a private eye, the jury figures he must have been there for some nefarious purpose and might expect to run into trouble. Anyway, I had no witnesses.

I dropped the check in my desk drawer and went back to bed. I was no longer taking the codeine and found it dull just lying there. I got up, took a long shower, hot and cold, and after I had dressed I felt pretty good. By some chance, they hadn't marked my face. There was plenty of stiffness and it was painful to breathe deeply, but I felt tighter and better organized inside.

I went over to Tony's and ordered a highball as an experiment. It was cool and quiet in there, ahead of the evening rush, and I sat with the cold glass on the polished bar and read the papers and made dull jokes with Paula, the early waitress. At five-thirty I moved into a booth and ordered a steak. It went down all right and stayed down.

Back in the office I fiddled around, looking at odd, meaningless scraps of paper, accumulated over a period of months. I decided to clean out my desk and got a start on it, but quit finally from boredom. The only constructive project left to me was to check with my answering service and I did it, convinced in advance there would have been no calls, but doing it for the sake of routine.

"There were three calls," the girl said, "from a woman who wouldn't leave her name. It seemed urgent. She said she would call again at eight-thirty."

"Anything else?"

"That's all."

"I'll be in the rest of the evening."

"All right."

I sat at the desk, waiting. In spite of myself, I began thinking about Sherry Turner. I had no reason in the world to think it was she who had called. It was extremely unlikely that Sherry Turner would call me. I had prepared many speeches against the time when she might and had thrown them all away.

By eight-thirty, I had managed to convince myself that she had been the caller. At eight-forty-five, I decided she had lost her nerve and wouldn't call again. The thought was interrupted by a gentle knock at my door.

"Yes?" I called.

A quiet female voice spoke through the panel. "May I come in?"

"Please do."

She wasn't Sherry Turner. She was a woman somewhere between fifty and sixty, with graying, well-groomed hair, dressed tastefully and conservatively in a plain dark suit and white blouse. She was the kind of woman that when she came into the room, you would stand up. And I did, and showed her to my most dignified chair.

5.

Her name was Catherine Colby. She was a school teacher. She had been in this line for most of her adult life and she was now principal of an elementary school in one of the far-out suburbs. She apologized for having come without calling again and I said that was perfectly all right. She was not my usual type of client and it would have been hard for her to do anything of which I could disapprove. She seemed to sense this, but didn't push it.

"I'm not here for myself exactly," she said.

That's an awfully old gambit in my business, but from her I accepted it.

"It affects one of my teachers." She paused. "Would it be all right not to mention any names until after we've talked for a while?"

"You tell it any way you want to."

"It's not that I don't trust you——"

"No reason for you to trust me."

"I don't know about that. Anyway, this girl is a good teacher. She has a little girl of her own——"

"She's married?"

"There was a time during the depression when married women didn't teach. Times have changed—thank God. This girl had left her husband, I don't know why. She went to school to get her credentials in shape and she was given a contract at my school for one year. It was renewed at the beginning of this term for another year. One more and she will have tenure." She paused again. "That means——"

I nodded. "It means she can't be fired."

"Not exactly. Gross misconduct or incompetence ——"

"I understand. She's in line for job security."

She looked away, frowning. "Yes, but she may not make it," she said. "She may not even complete this year."

"You said she has a contract."

"Contract or no." She exchanged the frown for a grim smile. "To put it bluntly, Mr.——"

"Call me Mac."

"All right—Mac. Someone is out to get her."

I sat up straighter and gave her some extra attention. It was like knowing that it will rain even though you haven't seen the clouds or felt the wind.

"Out to get her," she repeated slowly, "in an old, but still fashionable manner."

We looked at each other across the desk.

"Would you care for a slug of brandy?" I asked.

She seemed startled, then nodded quickly. "I think I would."

I went to the kitchen, got the bottle and a couple of glasses and brought them back. I was moving stiffly and as I poured into her glass I saw her watching me furtively.

"You're in pain," she said. "I shouldn't have come barging in this way——"

"It's nothing. It wasn't so good a couple of days ago, but it's better now. Occupational hazard."

We tasted the brandy and I said, "You people have occupational hazards too."

"Of many kinds."

"This teacher—do they have anything on her?"

"I can't imagine what it would be. She works hard and faithfully, gets on well with the other teachers. She lives a quiet life, has no so-called vices, major or minor." She smiled a little. "A major vice in our profession would be what we used to call 'carrying on.' Minor vices include smoking, gambling, using bad language, that sort of thing—or sitting around drinking brandy with private detectives."

"That last could turn into a major vice, if you let it get hold of you."

"I'll fight it."

"How did you know they were after her?"

She opened a black purse and took out two sheets of folded paper, opened them and slid them across the desk. The one on top was a circular letter on plain paper addressed to "Elementary and Secondary School Principals" of the district. It requested school officials to make a check on "supplementary reading matter" —books, periodicals, newspapers, etc.—brought from a teacher's personal library into the school. There was a request that in the event a check revealed that any teacher was making use of "questionable material," this fact should be reported to the Board of Education, with details.

"What do they mean by 'questionable material'?" I asked her.

She shrugged. "If they have to define it," she said, "they run into trouble. If you would ask them directly, you would probably get an answer like this, quote: 'I'm sure the vast majority of loyal American teachers understands what is meant by questionable material.' "

"Do you think that's true?"

"How could it not be true? And if it's true, what's the purpose of a directive like this? I don't mean to be naïve, but we've been pretty free of this sort of thing in my town, until recently." She waved her hand rather vaguely. "The trouble with a thing like this—it puts people on edge. You can destroy the strongest mind in the world if you question its judgment repeatedly for a long enough time. You could do it to Einstein!"

"Einstein is dead."

"I know."

I slid the top sheet aside and read the second. It was a letter addressed to Miss Catherine Colby, Principal of the Horace Mann School, and signed by someone named Rosslyn, Secretary to the Board of Education.

"Dear Miss Colby," it read. "With reference to the above-mentioned teacher—"

I glanced up, looking for the name, and saw that she

had pasted a strip of brown tape over a line near th top of the page; a line that might have read: "In re 'Somebody.' " I left the tape where it was.

". . . you are requested to furnish the Board of Education with information as respects the following:

"1. Said teacher's personal history; i.e., marriages, divorces, former dwelling places, family background, previous employment, etc., to the extent that this information is not included on said teacher's application for a position in this school district.

"2. Personal habits and associations of said teacher at the present time and in the past.

"3. Names of any and all organizations of whatever nature, including religious affiliation, of which said teacher is or has been a member.

"It is suggested that you interview said teacher in order to ascertain the requested information to the fullest extent. Your prompt attention is requested."

When I finished and looked up, she was watching me steadily. I poured another slug of brandy.

"The only thing I can think of that they left out," I said, "is how many times a day does she go to the toilet."

"If they had thought of it——" she said.

"What have you done about it?"

"I showed her the letter."

"And now you've shown it to me."

I got up and prowled stiffly around the desk.

"What did you think I could do about it?" I asked.

"I don't know. I thought there might be something."

"What can you do yourself?"

"Not much. I can make recommendations. I can

'select substitute teachers from an approved list. But I
can't write to the school board and say this teacher is
all right and please stop this nonsense. That is, I could
do it, but it wouldn't carry any weight."

"What did she say when you showed her the letter?"

"She looked me in the eye and said, 'I'll be glad to
tell you anything you want to know, Miss Colby.' "

"So——?"

"So I didn't ask her anything except how are things
going? and she said, 'Just fine,' and that was that."

"I'm not trying to back away from it," I said, "but
it seems to me that what she needs is a lawyer."

"I went to three of them. They all said the same
thing. Nothing has happened. There's nothing they
can do until some material has been developed."

"You think there's something to be developed?"

"There must be something. Everybody has something buried. Nobody is perfect. I'm not, God knows.
But I've been a teacher and an administrator for over
thirty years, starting in a one-room schoolhouse where
I had to haul my own coal to keep the place heated. I've
been a good teacher and I make a pretty good elementary principal. It wasn't always easy and I'm kind of
proud of it."

She fumbled through her purse. "I might cry a
little," she said.

"Go right ahead."

She blew her nose in a ladylike way, put the handkerchief away and tucked a loose strand of gray hair
up under her hat.

"There's another thing I'm proud of," she said. "I've
saved some money. Something over two thousand dol-

lars. I don't know how much it costs for a private detective——"

"Let's make sure I'm what you need. You said the girl was frank and co-operative. Why not just ask her whether there's anything in the past?"

"There are some questions I couldn't ask, school board or no school board."

"You mean that no matter how frank she seems, she's capable of holding out on some things."

"Certainly. And I too—and you."

Which was absolutely true.

"Suppose we should find something—what then?"

"Information about another person is only as good as the use people make of it," she said. "If someone is really out to get her, he'll make whatever he finds into something he can use against her. If we get it, we can make our own use of it, or at least present it in a full light—which could make quite a difference."

"Is there anything specific that you know of?"

"I know she's worried, under a strain. My best guess is it has something to do with her husband."

"They're not divorced?"

"Just separated."

I quit the pacing and went back to the desk.

"I would have to talk to her," I said. "Can you tell me her name now?"

"Of course. I don't know why I didn't tell you in the beginning. It's Kadek—Lorraine Kadek."

"Kadek," I repeated.

"That's her married name. Her maiden name was Jarvis."

"Kadek," I said again.

"K-A-D-E-K."

"I got it," I said.

I gave her another chance at the brandy, but she turned it down. She got out of her chair a little tiredly and moved toward the door.

"There's another way to go at this," I said, "that we haven't mentioned."

"What's that?"

"Very common procedure. Assuming someone is out to get her—we get something on him, whoever he is. When he sees what we've got, he backs down, gives up the fight. Nine times out of ten."

I watched her closely. Her eyes moved vaguely and after a moment she shook her head.

"I don't know," she said. "If there's to be a fight, I'll gladly fight. But I have to fight my way." She worked up a faint smile. "I used to be a pretty good fighter. But ever since Mr. Turner got on the school board——"

"Mr. Turner?"

"Roscoe Turner. He's a wealthy man—quite a big man in the community."

She saw something in my face.

"Do you know Mr. Turner?" she said.

"I've talked with him."

"About this—the school situation?"

"No, on a personal matter."

"Do you know him well?"

"Barely. I know something about him."

"Something he wouldn't want known?"

"I doubt that he's worried about it. The thing is— he knows who I am. If I turn up on the other end of an investigation in his home town, I might be useless."

She was silent, gazing around the room moodily.

"Or," I said, "it might work the other way around."

She brightened a little. "Of course it might!"

"I'll call you tomorrow," I said.

She frowned at that. "Very good. Perhaps the telephone conversation should be brief and—casual?"

"Have they got your office bugged?"

"Got it what?"

"Wired? Secretly? Are they listening in on you?"

"I don't think so," she said, "but I'm not sure. I'm just not sure."

She straightened her shoulders and came across with that smile. "As a teacher," she said, "I'm more or less of a warhorse. But as a woman, I'm not so tough any more."

"You're plenty tough," I said. "You went out on a skinny limb just coming to see me. By the way, how will you get back?"

"I have a car."

"Do you want me to follow you home?"

"No! I'm still tough enough to drive home. Thanks for listening."

"It was a pleasure."

She lingered at the open door.

"These days," she said, "I think everyone ought to have his own private investigator, don't you?"

She stood very straight and firm, with dignity, and not afraid of much. I liked her.

"You're plenty tough," I thought, and realized as I closed the door behind her, that I was saying it aloud.

I went to bed, slept and woke and lay, tense and dry

mouthed, unable to drop off. After a while I got up and
heated some milk, but when I tried to drink it, it tasted
like dissolved chalk.

In the office, I found myself browsing in the telephone
directory. There was a Karl Kadek listed. When I
looked at my watch, it read three o'clock. It was early—
or late—to go calling. But I wasn't growing any
younger and maybe I had a moral duty to warn this guy
that someone was out to get him, as well as his wife. If
I could pick up some information in the process—well
then.

6.

Kadek's address was ten minutes' drive north and
west, in a section of old brick apartment buildings,
long since converted to rooming houses. Here and there,
like a thin slice of bologna between two thick slices of
bread, you would find a narrow brownstone of three-
and four-story apartments. The one I wanted was like
all the others except that lights showed now at the
third floor of an otherwise dark mass of stone.

At this hour the street was quiet with the restless
city quiet that comes a couple of hours before dawn,
between the closing of the latest saloon and the coming
of the milkmen. A car now and then, a police prowl car,
the scream of a cat—these were the only sounds of life.

I parked half a block down from the building and sat there for a couple of minutes, trying to figure out why I had come. I could remind myself all right, with words. But I was simultaneously wide awake and drained of energy and none of it seemed important.

A prowl car drifted by and the spotlight jerked briefly in my direction, the beam passing and jerking again. They didn't stop. I didn't know whether it was because they had recognized me, because they were too tired to bother or because it was a quiet night. Anyway, their simple presence gave me a shot in the arm and I climbed out of the car and walked down to the building. It was recessed between the two flanking rooming houses and there were dark shadows over the twenty feet of cement and crab grass between the walk and the front door.

In the vestibule, there were six brass mailboxes set in the wall. The single name *Kadek*, in longhand, showed on a card under the box assigned to Apartment 3A. I pushed through the inner door and climbed the tired old stairs to the third floor.

Apartment 3A was at the front end of the third floor hall. A thread of yellow light showed under the door. I knocked and got no answer, waited and knocked again. I put my ear to the panel and heard a whisper of sound. A woman's voice said, "Who is it? Go away!"

I had heard that hoarse, frightened whisper before, in a dark alley behind a big hotel.

"It's Mac," I said. "I came to see Kadek."

There was some silence and when I lifted my hand to knock again, the door opened and she was standing there. I started in and she drooped toward me. I had to grab her to keep her from falling. Her fingers alternately clutched and slid over my coat. She was a badly scared little girl and she smelled like a recently drained beer keg.

I walked her across a blue-walled living room and tried to get her to sit down. She broke into the shakes. I clamped my hand over her mouth when she opened it to scream. She fought for a minute, then collapsed into the chair and began to cry quietly into her folded arm. She was sprawled awkwardly in the chair and I tried to adjust her dress over her thighs and knees, but without much success. She neither helped nor hindered me, which told me something.

"All right now," I said, "what's the matter?"

She couldn't tell me anything. She finally looked up and her lips moved, but she couldn't get the words out. Her face was tear streaked and her lipstick smeared on her mouth. Her hair was in a mess. When she tried to tell me about it, she started to shake again.

"Is Kadek here?" I asked her.

She just stared at me, shivering. I looked for something to put over her, but there wasn't anything in sight. I took off my coat and put that on her and started to look around the place.

It was a strange decor to find in such a building. It was an apartment such as you find often in my own neighborhood, inhabited by what passes in these times as the Bohemian set. Around there it wouldn't be unusual. But around there, too, the rents would be two or three times higher.

A small grand piano stood on a low platform in one corner. The furniture was modern, decked with brightly colored cushions. The ceiling was pink or coral. The two windows were covered by burlap curtains in two tones.

The room was unkempt, as after a party. There were glasses on a coffee table; an empty whisky fifth and a half-gallon wine jug, nearly empty. One of the glasses had tipped over and dribbled out a ragged stain on the blond table top.

A narrow hall led off the living room to the rest of the apartment. The bathroom door stood open on my right. This room, too, had been done in a somewhat fancy manner, with pictures of fish on do-it-yourself tile around the tub. There was a pile of used towels on the floor and water stood in the lavatory. The water was brownish red.

Across from the bath was the kitchen. It was a mess. Dirty dishes had piled up on the sinkboard and there were scraps from half a dozen meals. A couple of empty wine bottles stood on a shelf.

Two doors remained, one at the end of the hall, evidently leading to a closet, and one diagonally across from the kitchen door that would open on a bedroom. They were both shut. I went to the bedroom door and it was locked. When I put my ear to it, there was nothing to hear.

I felt—and smelled—the girl nearby and when I looked around, she was leaning against the jamb of the open bathroom door. Her eyes were watching me but her head was twisted into the room, as if she might break for the bowl at any moment. She held my coat with one hand by a sleeve and she was a real sick-looking kid.

"It's locked," I said.

She nodded stiffly.

"What's inside?"

She looked into the bathroom and scratched her back slowly against the doorjamb.

"Where's the key?"

She didn't answer, but her eyes flicked past me along the hall. I saw a key protruding from the lock of the closet door.

She dropped my coat and stumbled into the bathroom. I went to the closet and got the key. I picked up the coat and put it on, making sure everything I'd had was still in the pockets. Then I stuck the key in the lock, twisted it and pushed open the bedroom door.

A man lay on top of the bed, fully dressed, even to shoes. The bed had not been made up and the bedclothes were wadded and twisted under him. He was about five feet ten inches long and of stocky build, though not fat. He lay on his back with his face turned up and his features were broad and heavy, but ruggedly handsome. The fingers of his right hand were spread at the end of his sprawled arm and they were long and a little knobby, as if he had arthritis, or had spent a lot of time cracking his knuckles. He had stiff, red-brown hair, very thick, trimmed in a crew cut. There was a hole in his right temple, just below the hairline, about the size of a large pea. There was some blood on the side of his head.

I stood in the doorway, looking at him, then walked slowly into the room, past the foot of the bed and around to the other side. Draped on a chair were a pair of men's nylon pajamas and a woman's nylon negligee with puffed organdy sleeves. A pair of mules sat beside some men's slippers on the floor. On the chair seat lay a man's wallet. I flipped it open and looked at the identification card under the plastic window. The name on it was Karel Kadek. According to the ID card, he had been thirty-two years, four months and thirteen days old at approximately midnight, three and a half hours earlier—if he had lived that long.

I touched his left hand, which lay on his chest, and it was chilly and slightly stiff. I guessed that midnight might have been just about the time. I looked around the room some more, but there was nothing that told me anything. I put the wallet back on the chair and went out, locking the door.

7.

Sherry Turner was in the bathroom, leaning on both hands on the lavatory, staring down at the pool of red-brown water. I reached across her, got hold of the chain that held the stopper and pulled it out. The water bubbled slowly down the drain, leaving a faint, pink stain on the bowl. The last of it had run out before she turned her head slowly to look at me. Her eyes were slightly crossed. I hadn't noticed it that other night. Or maybe, that other night, they hadn't been crossed.

"Did he come at you?" I asked her.

She just blinked. I groped for a simpler way to put it. "Did you shoot him?"

"No," she said.

"Did he shoot himself?"

She moved her head, swinging it slowly away from me, then letting it swing back. "I don't know."

It was hard to look at her distorted face. When my eyes dropped, I saw some stains on the front of her gray dress.

"How old are you?" I asked.

"Twenty-two."

I started out into the hall.

"Why?" she said.

"Just for tonight, I wish you were seventeen. They're so much nicer to you in the juvenile division."

There was a telephone on a stand in the hall. I picked it up and the dial tone came over like the rasp of a working buzz saw. I tossed it from one hand to the other a few times and when I glanced around, she was in the bathroom doorway again, watching me. Finally I wiped the thing clean with my handkerchief and replaced it. Sherry disappeared in the bathroom.

I unlocked the bedroom door and went in, walked around the bed, avoiding him with my eyes, and picked up the negligee and mules. There was no closet, but a portable, curtained wardrobe stood in a corner. I pushed the curtain aside and looked at an assortment of masculine attire.

I carried the negligee and mules to the bathroom.

"Are these yours?" I asked her.

She looked at them and nodded.

"How long have you been here?"

"Since—Friday night."

"Is that why you ditched your bodyguard? So you could come to this place?"

Her voice thickened when she spoke and I had to strain to make out the words.

"I'm sorry about that—I had to get way from them. I'm sorry if they hurt you——"

"How long has he been in there like that?"

She met my eyes and tried to talk, but broke down. She nearly fell against the lavatory and I got her around the waist and walked her back to the living room. I sat her in a chair and put the negligee and mules on another.

"How long?" I asked. "Try to tell me what happened."

She worked on it and some of it came out. "I had to go out—to the drugstore. About midnight. When I came back, he was lying on the floor—right there. I didn't know what to do. There was blood on him."

Her throat jumped. I made a sign for her to speak quietly, but she couldn't.

"He wasn't dead!" she said. "He moved!"

I put my hand over her mouth and held it until she calmed down.

"You put him on the bed?" I asked.

She nodded. "I had to drag him—it took a long time."

"You didn't call anybody—a doctor—police?"

"I didn't know what to do. When I got him on the bed I thought he was dead. I couldn't make his eyes stay shut!"

I moved to stop her mouth, but she pushed my hand away, got control and whispered the rest. "I drank a lot of wine," she said.

"You went to the drugstore all alone, at midnight?"

"It was—something personal."

"Did you take a taxi?"

"No. There's an all-night drugstore around the corner."

"Had you ever been in there before?"

"No."

I looked at my watch. It was after four o'clock now. In about half an hour it would begin to grow light.

"Do you have anything else of your own here?" I asked. "Do you have a bag or anything?"

"At the end of the hall, in the closet."

I went down there and found an expensive, light-weight overnight bag, containing lingerie and toilet articles. A woman's cloth coat hung on a rack beside two dresses. On the floor, pushed back in a corner, was a fresh-looking paper sack. I hauled it out and it was the personal purchase she had made at the drugstore. I found room for it in the bag and folded the two dresses in on top. When I got the coat and bag back to the living room, she was chewing the knuckles of her right fist, staring at me.

I put the negligee and mules in the bag and snapped it shut. She was shivering again and I got the coat around her and made her put her arms in it.

"Is there anything else? Besides what I found in the closet?" I asked.

"No," she said around her fist.

"We have to make sure."

I went back to the hall, forced myself to enter the messy kitchen and looked around carefully. I saw nothing that seemed to belong to her, except lipstick stains on glasses. I checked the closet again, found nothing, made one more inspection of the bedroom, went through the key routine again and went on to the bathroom. A pair of nylon stockings hung on a hook behind the door. I looked through the pile of used towels and none of them had any monograms. They were cheap towels, such as a man might buy at a variety store.

I used the stockings to wipe off the doorknobs of the closet, bedroom and bathroom doors. I hadn't touched anything else that would show anything, except the two knobs on the front door. There was a large pocket in her coat and I stuffed the stockings into it, got hold of her arm and brought her to her feet. She stood, swaying a little, letting me adjust the coat on her shoulders. I picked up the bag, took her arm and led her toward the door. She hung back, pulling away.

"I have to go to the toilet."

"You'll just have to wait," I said. "It won't be long."

She put one finger in her mouth. "But I——"

I took her arm firmly and got her started again.

"Try to hang on," I said.

I pushed a wall switch and the room went dark. I got out my handkerchief, opened the door, wiped off the inside knob, got the door shut and the outside knob clean. I twisted it, checking, and the door was locked. So no casual acquaintance could barge in, looking him up. I had no way to check on how many might have keys.

She came along pretty well then down the stairs and outside. The milkmen had begun the rounds, but the only truck in sight was going away as we hit the sidewalk. There was no other traffic. I walked her quickly to the car, threw the bag in behind the seat, got her settled and the door locked beside her, climbed under the wheel and drove away from there. She sat stiffly in the seat, staring straight ahead, chewing on her fingers.

"Who is Roscoe Turner?" I asked her.

She took her fingers out of her mouth.

"My father," she said.

Pretty soon I asked, "That one back there—Kadek—was he married?"

"Yes."

"What did he do for a living?"

"He was a musician."

"Was he working at the hotel the other night when we were there?"

"Yes."

She leaned away from me and put her head against the window. "I'm sorry," she said. "I'm so awfully sorry——"

I let her be sorry while I drove back to my own neighborhood and got parked in front of the office. It was still dark.

8.

Inside, I showed her to the bathroom, opened her overnight bag on the bed and went out to the desk. I found the check from Roscoe Turner, put it in a clean envelope, sealed, addressed and stamped it. I knocked on the bathroom door and she asked what I wanted.

"I'm going across the street to mail a letter," I said. "I'll be right back."

"All right," she said.

The street was dark, cold and deserted. I dropped the envelope in the letter box outside Tony's joint and returned, drawing some deep breaths. Each one hurt.

When I got back, she was still in the bathroom, but she had made some use of the overnight bag and I sat down at the office desk to wait. After a few minutes I saw that the big front window had begun to lighten and I walked over and pulled the cord, closing the blind slats. Something told me to look around and she was standing in the bedroom doorway. She had changed her dress and washed her face and hadn't replaced any make-up. The good tan on her face was blotched with pallor, but her general appearance was better than it had been an hour earlier.

"What are you going to do?" she said.

Her voice was dull and hard, without hysteria, but also without life.

"I'm trying to think," I said. "Have you ever been fingerprinted?"

"No."

"Never, for any reason?"

"Not that I remember."

"Because there were a lot of glasses and bottles and dishes around there and you must have handled most of them some time or other."

She said nothing.

"You said you were there three days. Was there anybody else there, at any time, besides the two of you?"

"Nobody."

"You didn't have a party or anything—other people? Anyone who knows your name?"

"No."

"The only time you went out was to go to the drugstore?"

"No. I went to work with Karl every night."

"Karl?"

"His name really was Karel—K-A-R-E-L, but he shortened it to Karl for professional reasons."

"Where was he working?"

"At a place near Rush Street."

"I thought he worked with that hotel orchestra."

"That was a one-shot, on his night off."

"*Friday* was his night off?"

"They used a trio on Fridays."

"You went to work with him last night too?"

"Yes."

"And both of you got home by midnight?"

"He left work early. He didn't feel well."

She moved out of the doorway toward the sofa across from the desk. She was weaving and I managed to get over there in time to catch her and help her onto it.

"How much did you have to drink in the last three hours?" I asked.

"I don't know. A lot."

"Can you still feel it in your stomach?"

"Not much."

"Does the room shift on you when you close your eyes?"

"No."

I found her pulse and timed it roughly. It was pretty good, not too slow, but her skin was clammy and she trembled spasmodically. I put my arm under her shoulders and lifted.

"Come on," I said, "it's past your bedtime."

She held back. "Where——?"

"In the bed. Come on."

"In your bed?"

"It was made up clean today. I only used it for a short time——"

"I didn't mean that."

"Relax, Miss Turner. I'm in no condition to enter a wrestling match."

That brought her up and she let me lead her to the bed, where she sat down and began to peel off her stockings.

In the kitchen I poured a glass of milk and drank it. I put some more in a pan and set it on the stove. I found the box of codeine tablets, took one out and cut it in two with a knife. When the milk was warm, I filled a cup and took that with both halves of the codeine pill back to the bedroom.

She was in bed, covered to the chin, lying on her back, so that only her young, beautiful face showed in the darkened room.

I held her up while she took one of the half-tablets and drank some of the milk. She wanted both halves but I wanted her to talk some more and promised the rest for later. I pulled a chair up beside the bed and sat down and she watched me as from a distance, wary and catlike.

"Do you have to call me 'Miss Turner'?" she said suddenly.

Easy, kid, I thought.

"All right, Sherry. We're in this together, we might as well relax about it."

"We're in what?"

"Will you tell me something? When did you leave home?"

"A year ago."

"You didn't tell your father where you were living?"

"He found out some way——"

"You don't really have a fiancé in the army, do you?"

There was a pause.

"No," she said.

"Your father didn't want you running around with Kadek?"

"My father's a very proud man."

"He sent those two men out to keep you apart?"

"Yes."

"And you and I—we foxed them good, didn't we?"
She didn't answer. I heard the bedclothes rustle as she moved under them.

"Was this the first time you stayed with him?"

"Yes! I never went there before!"

"Take it easy. I'm just trying to figure out who there is to know about the two of you."

"There's nothing to know! Listen, I admit I was there; I stayed three days and nights. But nothing happened. Honestly, nothing happened!"

"I don't know. It seems to me something happened."

"I mean between us. Please believe me——"

"Oh. I'm not interested in a technicality. What happened was that Kadek got shot in the head and sooner or later he'll be discovered."

She gazed at me with her brown eyes. "It's just a—technicality to you?" she said.

"What are you talking about?"

She turned onto her side. Her eyes glistened in the dim lamplight from the office.

"You have to believe me. Nothing happened between us. I'm still——" She faltered on it.

"You're still a virgin. Good for you. It will go good with a jury."

"I'm not worried about a jury! I'm telling *you—personally!* Oh, God—" she turned her face into the pillow. "What you must think of me——"

"What I think of you doesn't matter. I'm working for you."

After a minute I tried again.

"Isn't there anything else you can tell me?"

I waited a long time. When she spoke finally, her voice was drowsy and distant.

"No," she said. Then later she said, "I wish I could. I really wish I could."

She had begun to cry and there were shiny streaks on her face. I gave it up.

"You'd better have the rest of that codeine and get some sleep," I said.

Her eyes shone damply as she took it and drank the rest of the lukewarm milk. I set the cup on the dresser. She lay very still, crying silently at the ceiling.

I got a couple of blankets from the closet and my dressing gown. As I started out to the office, she moved on the bed, looking for me.

"Mac—" she said quietly, "what are you going to do?"

"I'll have thought of something by the time you wake up," I said.

I thought of something right then. "One more question. Does your father send you money to live on?"

"No, I have an inheritance."

"Because whatever I think of, it will cost something. I don't know how much."

"I get fifteen hundred dollars a month from my mother's estate. She died five years ago."

"All right, Sherry. Try to get some sleep."

I heard her turn slowly under the bedclothes. I spread the blankets on the sofa, took off most of my clothes and got into the dressing gown, turned off the light and climbed in.

9.

Sleep came hard. Most of the bones and all the cartilaginous tissue of my thoracic cavity were on fire and there was no comfortable way to take it. I didn't want to take the codeine because I didn't want to oversleep and besides, for the next few days I would have to be on my toes. I lay there, shifting restlessly under the pain, watching the day brighten through the blind slats and I don't know whether I ever slept or not, but when I finally untangled myself from the blankets, I was able to move.

I got on my feet and looked at my watch. It was eight-fifteen in the morning. At the desk I pulled the phone onto my lap and dialed a number. It rang at the other end half a dozen times. The woman's voice that answered was husky with sleep.

"Good morning."

I told her who I was and the voice changed.

"Hello, Mac! Just up or still up?"

"Little of both. You busy, Georgiana?"

"You mean right now, or in general?"

"Well——"

"Fairly busy. I think the spiders must be crawling again."

That would be a reference to the vice squad.

"What've you got?" she said.

"I've got a paying guest for you; white female over twenty-one."

"Who wants her?"

I spoke slowly and distinctly. "Nobody that I know of yet."

There was a careful pause. Eventually she said, "When it breaks, will it be pretty hot?"

"It might."

There was another pause. I thought I heard bed-springs squeak.

"When do you want to bring her over?"

"Hour and a half?"

"Make it two hours."

I hung up, feeling better. Her name was Georgiana Hennessey and she had been known around the press-room at police headquarters as the "Three Star Final." She had been railroaded off the cops a few years before, though she was still a young, vigorous woman with plenty of know-how; an inside political deal based on a phony beef. In an incidental way I had uncovered some evidence that blew the beef apart, but they had bounced her anyway, to save face. Since then she had operated privately, much as I did, except that she specialized in domestic relations stuff and undercover work in department stores and offices. She ran a small ad in the Personals of the classified sections that read: "Let Georgiana Do It." She had stolen that from some radio detective series, but it was the only thing she had stolen in her life. We had been friends for some time. We had it in common about being bounced off the cops and besides, she was the friendly type, within limits. Now and then we threw business to each other. The business I was throwing her now could make life hard for her temporarily, if I had guessed wrong, but they tell me nothing is easy.

It wasn't easy to get up from the desk, tiptoe through the bedroom and climb into the shower. It was harder still to leave it after the cold water had braced me up. But somehow I made it and when I came out, the coffee had percolated to a deep black and Sherry Turner was awake and no longer crying.

We got through breakfast without incident and almost without conversation. She wouldn't meet my eyes. She spoke half a dozen words, such as, "Please," "Thank you," and "No, thank you." She seemed groggy and listless. Once she glanced up and must have seen some of the adhesive tape showing, because she winced and put her hand over her eyes. I didn't ask her any questions.

After breakfast I dressed in the office and she did

the same in the bedroom. Through the door I asked her to pack everything in her bag and when she finally opened the door, it was done. She was wearing the cloth coat. She had made up her face and fixed her hair and, except for the pale edges of her tan, she was almost as lovely as at the first time I had seen her.

When I took the bag from her, she looked at me directly for the first time.

"Where are we going?" she asked.

"I'm taking you to the home of a friend," I said. "Nothing fancy, but you'll be comfortable and more or less safe."

Her eyes wandered. "Maybe I should just go home, and wait. Sooner or later——"

"The later the better," I said, "but it's up to you. Would you rather go to your father's house?"

She shuddered under the coat.

"No."

"I thought it would be better for you not to be alone for a while."

She looked at me again, more deeply.

"What if I lied to you? What if I killed him?"

"I'm guessing you didn't."

She looked around the room.

"Well, why couldn't I just stay here?"

"There are several good reasons."

The young life was stirring in her again.

"Are you afraid, Mac?"

"Afraid of what?"

"You know what I mean."

"That's not a fair question, and I think you know it."

Her eyes fell.

"I'm sorry."

I opened the door and held it for her. She started out and the telephone rang. I swore under my breath. Sherry waited, half in, half out. It rang two or three more times and I beckoned her back in, went to the desk and picked the thing up.

"Yeah," I said.

The voice on the other end was grumpy and harsh. "Mac——"

"Yeah, Donovan."

"They give me a week off."

"Praise the Lord. How do you plan to celebrate?"

"I'm goin' up in the lakes and fish. You might want to come along."

"I'm on a case."

There was a disgruntled sigh. "Well, I hate to take all them muskies myself, but that's the way it goes."

"Sorry, Dad."

"Huh," he said. "You get your case cleaned up, come on fishin'——up around Minoqua."

"Okay. Have a good time."

"So long."

He hung up and I stood there, looking at the phone.

"Something wrong?" she asked from the door.

"I don't know. That was an old friend."

"You called him Donovan."

"That's right."

"Isn't he a policeman?"

"Best policeman I know. Greatest man in the world."

She seemed worried, though she tried to control it in her face.

"He's going fishing," I said.

"He wanted you to go with him."

"Yes."

"Why don't you go? I wouldn't want you to give up a fishing trip on my account."

I looked at her sharply, but she seemed to be sincere about it.

"I've some other work, too," I said. "I couldn't go now anyway. It's just that it's a bad time for Donovan to go fishing."

10.

Georgiana worked out of her home, a sprawling two-story house on the South Side. It was an anachronism among the modern apartments and commercial developments that surrounded it, but it was pretty good for her purposes. I think she had inherited it, along with enough income to pay the taxes, and she had had some wonderful offers for it in the last five or six years. But it came in handy as a place to put up clients temporarily. Many of these were unfortunate young ladies of one stamp or another and Georgiana had a mild Good-Samaritan complex. This had caused her to be taken a few times, but not often.

Sherry looked doubtfully at the house, but made no protest and I saw her do some quick primping as we climbed the steps.

There was a small card in the window with only

Georgiana's name on it. Her office was more like a doctor's or lawyer's than a private eye's—anyway, more like that than mine was. She had a waiting room with subdued lighting and tasteful decor, with good pictures on the walls and comfortable furniture. When you walked in, a bell tinkled faintly. It was pretty fancy, but I guess it paid off in her specialty.

Sherry stood like a dutiful child while I set her bag down and started toward the inner door. It opened before I reached it and Georgiana came out, carrying a cup of coffee on a saucer.

"Miss Hennessey," I said, "Miss Smith."

The name business was the only thing on which I had briefed Sherry. I had explained that it was necessary, not because we were trying to keep anything from Georgiana, but because she had to be innocent of the knowledge of Sherry's real name for her own protection. I had explained that this was not because Georgiana's protection was more important to me than Sherry's, but because if Georgiana were to be stripped of protection, she would no longer be useful to us. Sherry had apparently taken it all right. I picked the name "Smith" because it would be easy to remember for both of them.

Sherry and Georgiana said "How do you do" simultaneously and shook hands. I saw Georgiana's eyes work on her for the few seconds before she turned to me and guessed that she probably knew the girl by that time better than I did.

"Come on in," Georgiana said, "both of you."

We followed her into the office.

"Coffee?"

She had a glass pot full of it on a warming pan in one corner of her desk. It was good coffee and for a couple of minutes we all savored it and nobody said anything. This was a little rough on Sherry. Georgiana was studying her again surreptitiously and I felt I ought to say something to relieve the pressure, but I couldn't think of anything and it was Georgiana who came through.

"I love your hair," she said. "How do you make it stay that way?"

Sherry blushed and looked at her cup. "I don't know," she said shyly. "I guess it's the way it's cut."

"It's very good on you," Georgiana said.

Sherry looked up then. "I think yours is lovely too," she said.

I relaxed some.

After the coffee, Georgiana took us upstairs to a small suite—living-bedroom and bath—and left us alone. Sherry's mood brightened. There were two big windows overlooking a private park and if you looked carefully from the correct angle, you could see the lake, eight or ten blocks away. The furnishings were handsome, if not the latest, and on the way up we had passed a maid in a white uniform. So she could find it livable, if she could handle her recent memories.

"You'll be comfortable here," I said. "It's all right to go out, to a movie, or walking. But don't take a taxi. Walk or ride the buses. The main thing is to remember your new name and not to tell Georgiana anything, not anything at all about the last four days."

"All right."

"If we've slipped up somewhere, if the police should come here to talk to you, tell them nothing. Absolutely nothing. If they take you away with them, don't talk. They won't be rough with you if you keep still and don't talk snotty to them. If they take you away, Georgiana will call a lawyer. He'll be a good one and he'll know what to do."

"Yes, Mac."

"Try to keep your head and don't worry about things."

I had the door open. She came to me and stood very close, looking at me with those eyes. They were damn good eyes and they weren't crossed any more.

"Mac," she said, "I'm sorry about last night—the way I behaved——"

"Being sorry about things doesn't help either."

She looked hurt. I chucked her chin lightly.

"You're all right, Sherry," I said. "Some things won't be easy, now or later, but you'll make it."

She smiled fleetingly and leaned forward. Her lips brushed across my cheek. "Thank you," she said softly, "for everything."

I started out and she caught my sleeve.

"I almost forgot—you'll need money for all this." She fumbled with her patent leather purse.

"Not now," I said. "I can carry it for now. I'll make out a bill for you. Incidentally, don't write any checks. Have you got cash?"

She nodded. "I still have that hundred-dollar bill I had——"

"Let me change it for you. It will take care of you

for a while. If you run out, Georgiana will advance you some."

I gave her some tens and fives and she gave me the bill.

"When will I see you?" she asked.

"I'll be back. Maybe tonight."

"I'll wait till you come back. I won't go out."

"Whatever you think, but waiting for me might take some time."

I left her, went downstairs and knocked on the door of Georgiana's office. She opened it and nodded me in. As I stepped through the doorway, the outer door opened and a sad-faced woman of middle age came in, looking at us uncertainly. Georgiana smiled at her.

"Please sit down," she said. "I'll be with you in a minute."

The woman nodded and sat down. I went on in with Georgiana, who lit a cigaret and looked at me through the smoke.

"She's used to having things pretty fancy, isn't she?"

"She's a good kid," I said, "a little scared."

"She'll get to feeling fenced in. She'll want out."

"I told her it would be all right to go out. I gave her instructions. She's not to tell you anything. Likewise with the cops, if they come."

"Is it likely they'll come?"

"The honest truth is, I'm not sure. If they do, you don't know anything. I brought her here. Tell them that. You're just putting her up temporarily, because I told you she didn't have a place to stay."

"Anything to do in an incidental way?"

"If you can do it quietly, see what you can find out

about a piano player named Karl Kadek. Anything at all. Keep track of the expenses. Here's a bill in advance against everything."

Her eyes widened as she took it.

"You paying everybody off in bills nowadays?"

"Just today. The kid has enough change for a few days. She's good for whatever she needs."

"I believe that."

I looked back at her from the door. She looked good to me. Medium height, blond hair, carefully processed; sharp blue eyes, a good nose and chin. She was wearing a white blouse and a plain dark skirt. Policewomen are not selected for beauty of face and figure and Georgiana was no Helen of Troy. She was what you would call a good-looking woman. The duties and dress of police-women are not especially feminine and there was a certain mannishness about her. I had never discovered whether it was more than skin deep.

11.

It was a good hour's drive to Catherine Colby's suburb and by the time I reached the commercial section of the town, I was ready for lunch. I found a drugstore coffee shop with newsracks out front and went in there, taking the latest editions with me. There was no word in any of them about Kadek and I applied myself to a tuna fish salad and potato chips.

From a phone booth, I dialed the number of the city school district and after some shunting around, got connected with Miss Colby's office. A secretary told me Miss Colby was out to lunch. She invited me to come over there and wait, but I said I would wait at the drugstore and gave her the number of the public phone. Then I sat down at a nearby table, ordered coffee and studied my thumbs for half an hour.

The lunch-hour business dwindled to a couple of late eaters and it grew so quiet in the store, I could hear birds singing outside. When the telephone rang, a clerk in a white jacket headed for it and I waved him away and went in to take the call.

"One moment," the secretary said.

Miss Colby came on. "Is that you?" she said.

"Yes. What's new?"

"Nothing much."

"I thought we might have a cup of tea or something when you're through for the day."

"Delighted. Can you occupy yourself in the meantime?"

"Yes, if you'll direct me to the public library."

"It's on the corner of Fourth Avenue and Rosemead, not far from where you are."

"I'm trying to track down a rare book; I understand there's a copy of it in your library."

"That would be a little strange, but good luck."

"It's about fishing. The title is *Fighting the Big Muskelonge*. It's by a man named Donovan."

"Well, I hope you find it."

"I'm sure it's there. Where shall I meet you later?"

"I'll be leaving here around four-thirty. How about the Lakeside Inn at five o'clock?"

"I'll find it."

"I hope you find your book."

I paid my check, left my car parked across the street and walked about three blocks to Fourth Avenue. Half a block to my right, the library sat in the middle of a wide lawn.

It was small but comfortable and well lighted, doing a very slow business. I picked up a few magazines, took off my hat and sat down at the end of a table with my back to the desk. I could hear the two library workers carry on a desultory, *sotto voce* conversation. Once in a while someone would walk to the desk, ask something, return a book or take some out.

It was quiet in there and peaceful and I had to fight to stay awake. In a little while I heard heavy footsteps crossing the floor behind me. They came to a stop and one of the women at the desk said, "May I help you?"

I heard a guttural male voice. "I want a book named *Fighting the Big Muskelonge*, by Donovan."

Her slow reply was puzzled. "Donovan? Muskelonge? I've never heard of it. Just a moment, I'll check."

Her footsteps faded softly and I flipped over a couple of pages of a magazine. Pretty soon she returned.

"We don't have it, I'm sorry."

"Okay, thanks," he said.

"We can order it out from downtown, if you wish."

"No, no, thanks," he said quickly. "I'll be going to town myself. Thank you, miss."

The footsteps started away, heavy and plodding. I

waited till I heard them pause and the faint swish of the glass door opening, then picked up my hat, pushed back my chair and turned in time to see him moving away down one of the walks.

He was short and stocky, dressed in a gray suit and hat. The way he walked told me he would be about fifty years old. There was something familiar about him, but I couldn't have named him.

I was fifty feet behind him when he got onto the main sidewalk, went to a car parked near the corner and climbed in from the parking side without looking back. As he pulled away, disappearing at a moderate pace down the tree-lined street, I got a second reading of the license number.

Back at the drugstore, I dialed Georgiana's extended service number and after three rings she came on.

"How's it going?" I asked her.

"I haven't got much yet."

"Don't push it. How's the girl?"

"She hasn't left her room since she went into it. Probably moping about you."

"Uh-huh. Here's a license number." I gave her the number. "Will you connect it with a name for me?"

"Sure. You want a call?"

"Just hang onto it. I'll see you tonight."

"That's a promise?"

"Keep the coffee hot."

I looked up Lorraine Kadek's address in the directory and left the booth.

12

The fence around Mrs. Kadek's house was a white picket thing. A little girl with straight yellow hair, tied in two pony tails, was playing in the front yard. She had an orange crate there with some kind of cloth over it and dolls were set up around it on boxes and rocks. On top of the crate was a doll type meal of sand and grass and water in little tin dishes. She had everything under control. As I walked up, she was telling one of the dolls to sit up straight and keep her elbows off the table, and she wasn't getting any back talk.

I stood at the gate, watching her, and when she saw me suddenly, as she made a turn around the orange crate table, she stood very still for a count of three. Then she smiled. I leaned across the gate and she came forward slowly, wary but unafraid. She was maybe four years old.

"You want to come to the party?" she asked.

"It would be a pleasure, but we haven't been introduced."

She cocked her head and the pony tails jiggled.

"My name's Trudy. What's yours?"

"Mostly they call me Mac."

She pointed to the house next door.

"Is that where you live?"

"No, but I'm beginning to think I'd like to."

She turned away suddenly, bent and started pulling

at some daisies and geraniums growing in the yard. When she straightened up, she had a fistful of them. She brought them to the gate, holding them out.

"You want some flowers?" she said.

I took them. "Thank you," I said. "Is your mother home?"

"You mean 'Raine? No. Esther's home. 'Raine's at school. I don't go to school. Not till next year."

"That's soon enough."

Abruptly she turned away and ran by a narrow path toward a corner of the house, yelling, "Esther! There's a man here——!"

She disappeared and I pushed through the gate. One of the dolls looked up at me crookedly as I passed. She seemed serene and untouched by the heat of the day, which was considerable for early spring.

Trudy came flying back with pony tails waving.

"Come on!" she said. "Esther's back here——"

She ran ahead and I followed her along the path, around the house and toward the back yard, fenced along this side and screened by high shrubbery, some of which I had to duck under. Trudy didn't have to do any ducking. She ran hard and fast with every muscle working and won the race going away.

The back yard was a sixty-foot square of lawn, with borders of flowerbeds at the base of the fence and along the back wall of the house. There were a couple of trees. Near them stood an old-fashioned, three-seated swing suspended from an iron frame. A weathered hammock hung between the two trees and in it lay a woman of about thirty, sun-bathing. Trudy ran to her, tugging at her arm.

"Esther—there's a man to see 'Raine."

The woman raised her hand to shade her eyes and looked at me where I had stopped a few feet away.

"Hello," she said.

I held out the flowers Trudy had given me.

"I seem to have these. Maybe we ought to put them in some water."

"Trudy," she said, "go get something to put them in."

Trudy looked as if I had betrayed her, as, in fact, I guess I had.

"They're for *you*," she said.

"I thank you," I said, "and I'll be glad to have them. But we might keep them fresh while they wait."

She scowled and pooched her stomach out at me. I saw a bare strip of it where her sunsuit halter failed to join her shorts.

"*Flowers* don't have to wait," she said.

The woman spoke more sharply. "Trudy, get something to put them in. Take the flowers with you."

Still scowling, Trudy grabbed the flowers and ran to the house. I heard a screen door slam. The woman named Esther started to raise herself.

There is no graceful way to get out of a hammock, even under ideal conditions. I guess she did the best she could with it, but she was a big girl, she was dressed in a two-piece sun outfit and she wasn't very careful. After she had her bare feet on the ground, she didn't seem fussed. She gave a perfunctory tug to her brief shorts, hitched up the snug halter bra and nodded at me with what must have been a smile.

I couldn't be sure. She was tall, leggy and big-boned.

Her figure was good: generous in the chest and hips, with a small waist; and her legs, though long, were almost perfectly formed. But she must have been near the end of the line when they gave out faces. Not that hers was misshapen, or blemished. It was just that, as a combination of features, it failed noticeably to come off. It was what you might call a horribly plain face. Her nose was too prominent, her cheeks angled toward her chin, instead of curving and there was a squint to her eyes. It gave her a sort of perpetual, unpleasant frown.

"I'm Esther Jarvis, Lorraine's sister," she said. "Lorraine hasn't come home from school yet."

"Would it be inconvenient for me to wait?" I asked.

She moved her head and the squint was more obvious.

"I don't think I caught your name," she said.

"Sorry. I told the little girl. The name is Mac."

"Mac what?"

I told her my full name as it had been given to me roughly forty years before. It sounded unreal, as if it should belong to someone else.

"You're not from the Immigration Service?" she said.

I shook my head. "I'm a friend of Miss Colby's. I wanted to talk to Mrs. Kadek——"

Her face twisted with sudden anger. "Why don't you leave the poor kid alone?" she said. "Hasn't she had enough?"

She stalked away to the swing. The old, rusted springs squeaked. She sat with her elbows on her knees and her face in her hands.

"I guess either you or I didn't understand," I said. "I'm here to try and help Mrs. Kadek——"

"Sure," she said through her fingers. "Everybody wants to help little Lorraine."

She took her hands away from her face, but didn't raise it or look up.

"I'm sorry I intruded on your rest," I said. "I'll come back later. Or maybe I could catch her at school——"

She looked up quickly then. I had started to back off and she shook her head rather desperately and brushed her thin, brown hair back from her forehead.

"I didn't mean to be rude," she said. "Of course you may wait for her."

She was changeable, or scared. Probably both. A girl with so many assets, crowned by that one prominent liability, would likely be mixed up.

The screen door banged and Trudy came out, balancing a plastic jar with the flowers in it. She carried it way out in front, stiffly, in one hand. She was within ten feet of the swing when trouble struck in the form of an abandoned golf ball, half hidden in the grass. Her right foot made a direct connection. The flowers flew into the air and floated down. The jar fell to the ground, water splashed and Trudy yelled. She yelled loud and long and when I got to where she lay on the grass, kicking her feet against the ground, the yelling was as good as any I had ever heard.

She wouldn't have any help. When I touched her shoulder, she jerked away, rolling over in the grass and kicking now at the air. I glanced at Miss Jarvis, who sat in silence on the swing, watching us. Aunt Esther, I decided, had been through this before.

I picked up the plastic vase and some of the flowers

and reinserted them. The nearest source of water was a garden hose coiled at the back wall of the house. Kneeling beside it, having adjusted the tap, I found myself looking at the lower wall of the house, where a telephone line entered. There was a porcelain insulator set in the wall at the level of the floor joists and the line circled the insulator and curved out in a double loop above it, which was normal enough.

Two things about it were not normal. For one thing, the lead-out line was too thick, too new and shiny. For another, there was an extra line that the telephone company could have no use for. It descended from the insulator down the concrete foundation of the house and disappeared. I reached behind the flowers and found how the descending wire had been pegged into the ground. When I scraped some of the dirt away, I saw that at the ground level, it ran along the foundation toward the back steps and driveway beyond. It had been pegged down at intervals and dirt had been thrown over it lightly as far as the steps.

The steps were of wood, high and open, with space enough under them for a good-sized man, if he would jackknife some.

13.

When I got back to the swing with the refilled vase, Trudy's yells had diminished and she was simply cry-

ing, forcing it a little, I thought. Her aunt sat on the
swing, regarding the girl stonily. Trudy scowled at the
vase and rubbed a hand over her muddied face.

"All fixed," I said.

She turned away and let out a soul-shattering sob.

"Trudy," her aunt said, "you'd better go in and wash
your face."

Trudy sat stiff and silent, looking away from us.

"Go wash your face," Miss Jarvis said sharply.

Trudy wheeled onto her knees and shook her finger.

"I won't!" she screamed. "You're not my mother and
I don't have to do what you say."

Aunt Esther rose slowly and Trudy backed away on
her knees, screaming, "You're not my mother! You're
not my mother!"

I set the vase on the grass. Esther Jarvis kept ad-
vancing and suddenly Trudy scrambled to her feet and
ran off toward the house. The screen door banged
loudly. Esther tugged again at her shorts, but it didn't
help much. She looked awfully naked.

"What would you have done if she had held out?" I
asked her.

She shrugged her wide shoulders. "I don't know. I
wouldn't have hurt her. It's not my province."

It sounded stuffy and bookish.

"Would you like a cup of coffee?" she said.

"Sounds good."

She headed for the back steps and I followed. She
was something to follow. When she started up to the
door, I paused.

"Have you had any telephone service men out here
lately?" I asked.

"No. Why?"

"Mind if I take a look under your steps?"

She descended slowly, staring at me. I found that when she concentrated, her eyes nearly straightened out.

"Go ahead," she said. "Be my guest."

I crawled under from the driveway side to save the flowers and found a wooden box the size of a cigar box, attached to the inside of the far riser support of the steps. I got hold of it and pulled it free. It had been hooked by a single nail. I let it lie where it had fallen, went back to the other side and retrieved it. Miss Jarvis knelt beside me, so close I could feel her breath on my neck.

"What is it?" she asked.

I tapped the dangling wire and pointed out where it ran along the foundation of the house to the telephone conduit.

"The box is a radio transmitter," I said, "a pretty good one, I guess. The wire runs to your telephone."

I glanced at her and she was looking at me, not at the box. At that moment she lost her balance and I reached out to help her. She reached at the same time and our arms got tangled up. When she got steadied, with her thigh braced against mine, she relaxed her hold on my coat where she had grabbed it. But her arm remained across my back, as if for additional support.

"You mean our telephone has been tapped?" she said.

"I would say it has."

"But who———?"

Her fingers dug into my back, relaxed and dug again. It could have been a reaction to the disturbing news, but it felt, too, like a kind of harsh caress. I couldn't think of a graceful way out. She was locked against me and I was sure that if I should move, she would fall over.

I hefted the box with one hand.

"It's battery operated," I said, "heavy duty type. It would probably last a couple of weeks. They could pick up from it clear across town."

She said nothing. I felt her body leaning against me and my own sweat running coolly down my sides.

"You want me to disconnect it?" I asked.

"Hell yes," she said. "I mean naturally. That's an awful thing——"

I got out my pocket knife and sawed through the heavy black wire. It took some time and she stayed, watching, holding onto my coat.

I pushed the cut end of the wire back into the dirt, reaching awkwardly with one hand. The screen door squeaked and Trudy was looking down at us. She had not only washed her face, she had changed her clothes. She wore a yellow dress with a starched, flared skirt and a white sash. On her feet were yellow socks and patent leather slippers. The sash had not been tied and the shoes were unbuckled, but she was decent. She pointed solemnly.

"What's that?" she said.

Miss Jarvis straightened to her feet. I did the same, holding the box with both hands.

"It's a box with wires in it," I said. "It's like a radio."

"Can it make music?"

"It might, if you wanted it to," I said, "but I'm not much of a musician."

I saw Esther Jarvis stiffen in the act of tying Trudy's sash, and turn slowly to look at me with that squint. I hadn't meant anything special by it. Maybe I had put a strange emphasis on the word "musician," or maybe she was oversensitive to the word itself. She turned the girl around, buckled the shoes, gave her a light spat on the bottom and told her to go play with her dolls.

Trudy started to holler and her aunt picked her up and set her on the grass. I felt useless and off base, standing there with the box. The kid held out for a few seconds, then turned and ran off around the house, yelling. Miss Jarvis spread her hands.

"Honestly," she said, "sometimes——"

"About the box," I said, "for certain reasons, I'd like to hang it back where it was. It's no use to them now and I'd like it to be there later."

"Whatever you say," she said. "I'll start the coffee."

Inside the house, the telephone was ringing. I got under the steps, hung the box on the nail and coiled the wire up out of sight. When I went up the steps and knocked on the screen door, I could smell the coffee.

"Come in," she called.

I crossed a service porch into the kitchen, a roomy, clean place with a snack booth in one corner. She had set out two cups and saucers and some cream and sugar. I sat down in the booth and pretty soon she brought the pot over and poured from it.

"Lorraine just called," she said. "She won't be home for a while."

She seemed pleased about it.

"The coffee smells good," I said.

"I imagine you drink a lot of coffee. You must keep pretty irregular hours."

"Irregular hours?"

"You're a detective, aren't you?"

"Since we're discussing it——"

"I finally remembered who you are. You must have thought I was stupid."

"Not at all. The coffee is very good."

"I think it's only fair to warn you, you won't get anywhere with Lorraine."

"Get anywhere?"

"I've been telling her for a year to divorce him. But she has some idea about loyalty——"

"About whom are we talking?" I said.

She blinked once.

"Her husband—Karl Kadek." She shrugged her big shoulders. "Well, I guess it's too late now."

I set my cup down and looked through the window at the flowers in the back yard.

14.

When I looked at her again, she was pouring some more coffee.

"Too late?" I said.

"It's too late to do her any good in this school business. If they want to get rid of her, they'll do it."

"Who do you think wants to get rid of her, and why?"

She gave me another of those expansive shrugs. "Some people see a traitor behind every bush. You know what's been going on——"

"Is Kadek a Communist?"

"Certainly not! And neither is Lorraine——"

She broke off abruptly, setting her chin against me.

"You mentioned the Immigration Service," I said.

"Did I?"

I drank some coffee. After a minute, she seemed to feel called upon to explain.

"All right," she said, "I'm what they call an unfriendly witness. I'm afraid to talk about it, even to you."

"I don't blame you."

"Besides, she's my own sister!"

"I understand."

There was some silence.

"Listen," she said suddenly, "this telephone thing—how could they do that? They have to connect things up, and I'm here every day——"

"All day long?" I said. "Every day? Don't you go to the store—go shopping, with the little girl?"

"Yes, but we wouldn't be gone more than——"

"How long?"

"Not more than an hour, maybe two hours——"

"It would take about five minutes to install the box under the steps and lead the wire to the phone outlet."

"But don't they have to get inside, to the phone?"

"I came in just now through the back door. For a man who knows how, it would take about thirty seconds to get through the lock without leaving a trace. Or it could be done another way."

"How?"

"If there were two of them. Have you had any door-to-door salesmen lately?"

"They're around every other day with something. Most of them never get in the house."

"But once in a while——?"

She looked away.

"Well," she said reluctantly, "once in a while——"

"All right. One of them comes to the front door with his sample case. He gets in——or he works from the porch, ties you up with a long pitch. The second one is around in back, inside, wiring the telephone, and you never knew a thing about it."

She stared at me. "That's awful," she said. "When I think how easy it is——what a person might say over the phone, no matter how innocent——"

I let her dwell on it some.

"You think it's because of her husband that your sister is being hounded?" I asked.

"It has to be. There's nothing else in her life. Believe me, I know."

"You've been taking care of the house and the little girl for her?"

"Ever since before Trudy was born. She's always needed somebody to clean up after her. Even when we were kids, I spent most of my time taking care of Lorraine."

"Doesn't leave you much life of your own, does it?"

For the first time, behind her protective wall, I saw some of the pain in her. It showed in her strange eyes, softened them. It was real, tangible. I could almost have touched it with my fingers.

"When you're the older sister and you don't have a normal future," she said, "you take care of the younger ones. When our folks died, I got a job, helped her through school. I was a secretary, a pretty good one——"

She broke off, picked up the coffee pot.

"More coffee?"

"No, thank you. I have to be going."

"Aren't you going to wait for Lorraine? It won't be long——"

"Maybe I can see her later, in the evening. I have an appointment with Miss Colby."

She ran her fingers slowly over one side of her face. "Just one more cup?" she said.

"I wish I could. It's wonderful coffee."

Her shrug this time was less definite. It had an involuntary rhythm, like a reflex. "I'm not a bad cook," she said, "and housekeeper. I was a good secretary too. But that's no life. Sooner or later you have to start running around the desk—the old wrestling match."

I was standing now, looking down at her and she glanced up, catching my eyes unexpectedly. Bitterness flared in hers.

"Does that seem so strange to you?" she said. "That I should have wolf trouble?"

"By no means."

She pushed to her feet and started away toward the front door. She didn't bother to yank at her shorts. We had nearly reached the door when it opened and Trudy came in. She was crying again, but quietly, holding one hand tightly with the other.

"What's the matter, honey?" Esther said.

Trudy held up her hand. "I cut it——"

There was a scarlet stain on her forefinger. She put an arm around one of Esther's long legs and hid her face against it. Miss Jarvis put her hand on Trudy's head and patted it, rumpling the hair.

"I almost forgot the flowers," I said.

Trudy straightened. "Where'd you put them?"

"In the back yard."

She ran off like a fawn toward the back. Esther turned slowly, watching her go.

"Great kid," I said.

"I guess things get evened out," she said slowly. "When we were kids, I had to share everything with Lorraine—dolls and things. Now she's sharing her doll with me."

"Does her father ever come to see her?"

Her face twisted again, as earlier, in the kitchen.

"As far as she's concerned, her father is dead."

I heard the sound of Trudy's feet pounding back through the house. She stopped in front of me, breathless, holding up the vase. I lifted the dripping flowers and wrapped my handkerchief around the stems.

"I thank you," I said.

I got the door open. Trudy held up her wounded hand suddenly.

"Look, I cut it," she said.

She held it as high as she could reach. I glanced at Miss Jarvis, then leaned down and kissed the finger. It was bloody, a little dirty, and damp from the sweating vase. But it didn't taste bad. It tasted pretty good.

I went out and down the walk to my car. When I looked back, Miss Jarvis was standing on the porch and Trudy was leaning against her legs, waving.

15.

The man in the gray suit was climbing out of his car when I passed the graveled parking area of the Lakeside Inn, a rambling, roadside restaurant and cocktail lounge on the town's city side. I still couldn't place him at this distance, but so far, the predictions were running pretty good.

I drove back to town and parked in front of the Suburban Telephone Company. Like the library, it was a modern building with plenty of glass and a spacious reception room in cool green and coral. There was a counter along one wall with out-of-town directories and they furnished pads and pencils for making notes. A row of booths ran along the next wall at right angles. Beyond a low glass partition were rows of desks, deserted at this hour, but a girl sat at a reception desk in the angle formed by the counter and the booths. Across the room was a smaller counter framing an alcove and a sign over it read: SERVICE DEPARTMENT.

I looked up the number of the Lakeside Inn, went into the booth farthest from the girl's desk, and dialed.

A bartender answered. I could hear the clinking of

glasses as background to his voice. When I asked for Miss Catherine Colby he told me to hang on. I hung on for about five minutes. Finally she came on.

"This is Mac," I said. "Now you say, 'Oh yes, where are you?' "

She played it nicely. "Oh, yes, where are you?"

"We have to change our plans. Now you say, 'I see, what do you suggest?' Speak right up with it."

"I see," she said strongly. "What do you suggest?"

"From now on just answer 'yes' or 'no.' Okay?"

"Yes," she said.

"Is Mrs. Kadek with you?"

"No."

I hadn't counted on this and lost my voice for a moment. "Did she get cold feet?" I asked finally.

There was a long pause, then she said, "Yes."

But it could have meant "maybe."

I groped through my mind for an intelligent question that she could answer by yes or no. Try it sometime, Senators.

"Do you think she went home?" I asked.

Another pause and she said, "No."

I knew this question and answer routine had broken down.

"You're being watched, possibly overheard," I said. "Don't be alarmed."

After a moment she said, "Yes."

I could take that either way.

"Can you leave your house by a back door, cross the adjoining lot and come out on the next parallel street?"

"Yes."

"I would like for you to drive home, park on the

street and go inside. Wait till exactly six o'clock, then go out the back way to the next street. I'll pick you up. Will that be all right with you?"

"Yes."

"Now say, 'I'll wait for you at home.' "

"I'll wait for you at home."

"You're a good girl. You are now permitted to say good-by and to hang up."

"Good-by."

The phone clicked at the other end. I hoped that if anyone had listened in, he was suitably confused. I also hoped that confusion was growing in other quarters. I thought I could help it along.

At the counter again, I looked up Catherine Colby's address and made a note of it. I started out, then turned back and strolled toward the Service desk. It was unmanned and I had nearly reached it when the girl at the reception desk called across the quiet room.

"May I help you, sir?"

I walked over there and turned on my innocent smile.

"Well," I said, "I feel like a busybody, but you might appreciate knowing——"

Her voice was formal and precise. "We'll be glad to be of service."

"I'm a friend of Miss Catherine Colby's, Principal of the Horace Mann School. That's on—is it Third Avenue——?"

She was writing on a pad.

"I know that location. What is the service problem?"

"I don't know exactly. I called her today and got a very bad connection—noisy, you know? I could barely hear her. I don't know much about these things, but it just seemed to me there must be something wrong at her end—loose wires or something——"

"I see."

"I've always admired the Telephone Company for its fine service," I hastened to say. "Matter of fact, I own considerable stock. Miss Colby is a considerate person, not the type to complain, and you know how long it takes to get things done through the regular channels—Board of Education and all that."

"There wouldn't be any problem there. We service the school telephones directly, on a call from the person in charge."

I backed off.

"Thanks very much," I said. "If a man should go out the first thing in the morning, he could probably fix it in a jiffy."

"I'll see that it's reported, sir. Thank you for calling it to our attention."

She was a well-trained, nice-appearing girl of twenty-five, writing busily on a pad. As I reached the door, she called, "Would you mind letting me have your name, sir?"

I didn't like to be rude to her, but I went on as if I hadn't heard. Except for the slight rudeness, things were going fine. It was almost fun—like deliberately crossing wires as a practical joke.

Some joke . . .

At one minute to six I drove through an intersection half a block beyond Miss Colby's house. From the corner I could see the guy's parked car a few doors up from her place and across the street.

As I nosed around the turn at the next street, she stepped onto the sidewalk, looked both ways, then walked slowly away. I let her get to the next corner before pulling into the curb. When I opened the door, she glanced in, then nodded and got in beside me. I drove away from the neighborhood rapidly.

"Did you find your book at the library?" she asked.

"There's no such book," I said. "I made up the title as we talked on the phone. But I had been in the library only half an hour when a man came in and asked for it."

She said nothing.

"The same man was watching you at the Lakeside Inn and he is now parked in front of your house."

She stared through the windshield.

"I don't like that," she said. "I'm afraid it's making me angry."

"Then your reaction is normal. What about Mrs. Kadek?"

"I don't understand her attitude," she said. "After you called today I told her how I had gone to see you and why and invited her to meet with us. She said she was grateful, but she put me off, said she had a lot of things to do after school and that she just couldn't do it today."

"Did you press her at all?"

"A little. She asked me what the date was today and when we got that straightened out she said maybe we could get together on Friday."

"She gave no reason for putting it off?"

"None. I was a little exasperated. I've been thinking perhaps we ought to call the whole thing off."

"It's up to you, but I think you ought to know they've tapped into her home telephone."

She turned quickly, looking at me across the seat.

"I'm sure she doesn't know it."

"If it were mine," I said, "I'd want to know."

After a moment she said, "If I know her as I think I do, we can probably catch her at the school. If you want to turn right at the next corner——"

"I don't want to push you. I reported what I'd found."

"We'll go to the school," she said. "I'm still the boss around there."

There was a pretty firm set to her chin and I made the right turn.

"Does she always work overtime like this?" I asked.

"Quite often. I worry about it sometimes. I admire competence and industry, but dedication is a tricky thing to handle."

"Is she bucking for a promotion?"

"I don't think so, though I wouldn't object to that. I think it's what they call overcompensation. It happens to teachers—trying to make up in the classroom for the children they never had."

"Mrs. Kadek had one——"

"I know."

"Anyway, if she should lose her job through this investigation, it could be devastating to her."

"I should think. You'll want to turn left here."

I made the turn.

16

Long evening shadows fell across the green lawn and wide walk leading to the school entrance. As we walked toward the low, modern building, Miss Colby glanced around with proprietary interest.

"I'm lucky, you know," she said. "At least we don't have a classroom shortage."

"It's a rich town."

"Sometimes I feel it's a little too rich for my thin old blood."

There wasn't much I could say to that.

Inside was the odor of waxed linoleum and wood and paper. The corridors were deserted and silent, but far down on our right, light showed through the glass panel of a classroom door. Miss Colby led me down there.

The panel was on eye level and looking through it, we saw a young woman across the room, pinning children's drawings on a long wallboard. Miss Colby knocked and I followed her into the room as Mrs. Kadek turned, somewhat startled.

She was a good looking blonde of twenty-six or twenty-seven with fair, delicate skin and rather precise features, saved from sharpness by a well rounded chin and a slight enlargement of the bridge of her nose. Her eyes were gray and on the shy side, and as she faced us now, her hands were clasped so tightly that the knuckles were pale and the fingertips brightly pink.

Miss Colby introduced us, explaining, "After talking

with him again, I took it on myself to bring him here. I hope it's not too great an intrusion."

Mrs. Kadek looked at her hands. "Of course not," she said quietly.

She moved toward her desk and we joined her, standing. The rest of the room's furniture was strictly for the junior set.

"Miss Colby tells me," I said, "that the school board is digging into your past."

She leaned on the desk, her hands pressed flat on its top.

"Well," she said, "I suppose they have that right."

"That is by no means certain," I said. "A contract is a reciprocal agreement, regardless of the parties to it, including the government. There's no reason they couldn't have done the investigating before the contract was offered."

She said nothing, but glanced furtively at an inexpensive wrist watch. Aside from the shyness in her eyes, she looked like a successful career woman in a difficult and, currently, hazardous career. I thought we ought to be able to have a sensible conversation about a soluble problem, but there was a wall between us and I didn't know who or what had helped to build it.

"Is there anything in your life, Mrs. Kadek," I asked, "that could be twisted to make you look bad?"

"I suppose anything can be twisted," she said. "But why would anyone bother? Don't you think we're exaggerating the menace?"

I tried to catch her eyes, but they shifted.

"I found a gadget hooked onto your telephone today," I said.

She stood very still, waiting.

"I cut the connection. Some people take the attitude that if you're respectable and law-abiding, you have nothing to hide, so what's the difference if somebody listens in. I don't feel that way. I resent it. I guess I took it for granted you would too."

"Naturally I do."

"As for the menace of this investigation," I said, "it's true that it's not being conducted by some psychotic legislator. I have a hunch it's a one-man operation with a personal motive and it may die a natural death."

She faced me suddenly and spoke with a stiffness that took me by surprise. "Then it seems to me that we might just let it die."

I glanced at Miss Colby, who seemed very neutral. I decided I didn't know her well either. Still, she had engaged me and until she should call me off, I guessed I might as well go on with it.

"Could we talk for a minute about your husband, Mrs. Kadek?"

"What would that have to do with——?"

"I don't know. I have to start somewhere. You're not divorced from him?"

"No."

"How long have you been separated?"

"Over a year."

"When did you last hear from him?"

There was a considerable pause.

"Quite a long time ago."

"Was he a citizen, Mrs. Kadek?"

"A citizen——?"

"Of the United States."

Miss Colby was frowning.

"No," Mrs. Kadek said, "but there's no secret about it. It's on my application——"

"Please don't be upset," I said. "I'm fishing."

"He came in on a student visa," she said, "and took out first papers several years ago. He was from Central Europe and he had been studying in Cuba."

"Cuba?"

"You can get a very good musical education in Cuba. Many people don't know this."

"I'm glad to know it. Did you marry him after he took out first papers, or before?"

"Afterward."

"So the marriage had nothing to do with getting him into the country, or his citizenship——"

"Absolutely nothing."

"But it would be a good thing for him to be married to an American citizen, in case anything should come up."

She turned away sharply. She was quite red in the face. "I suppose it would," she said.

"Is that why you haven't divorced him?"

The fingers of her right hand opened and closed spasmodically. "I don't see what it has to do with this—other matter," she said. "I wish we could just forget the whole thing!"

I kept quiet. There was the distant slam of a door and a moment later, running footsteps in the corridor outside. We all looked around as the classroom door swung open and Trudy ran in, calling, " 'Raine! We came to get you——!"

Then she saw Miss Colby and me and stopped abruptly. After a moment she went on shyly to Mrs. Kadek, who leaned down to gather her in.

I glanced at the door and saw Esther's unfortunate face looking in at us through the panel. When I looked at her she disappeared quickly and didn't come on in. Trudy was tugging at her mother's arm.

"Come on! Supper's ready. It'll get cold!"

Mrs. Kadek straightened, holding the little girl's hand.

"Aren't you going to say hello to Miss Colby?"

Trudy made the long look upward to Miss Colby, who smiled at her.

"Hello, Trudy."

"Aren't you ready yet?" she said impatiently to her mother.

"Yes, I'm ready. We'll go now."

Trudy looked at me. "What did you do with the flowers?" she said.

"They're in my car. I'll take them home."

"Be sure and put them in water," she said sternly.

"Yes, ma'am."

As I moved to the door with Miss Colby, Lorraine Kadek met my eyes.

"I'm sorry," she said. "I know you were only trying to help me."

"I hope I can," I said.

Miss Colby murmured something and we went out. Walking down the corridor, we passed Esther Jarvis, tall and lonely looking against the wall, her head twisted into shadow. I nodded and spoke and after a while she said, "Hello."

Her voice was distant and flat and when Miss Colby greeted her, she made no answer. As we reached the high front door, I heard her crossing the corridor and her voice again, sharp and insistent, and her sister's reply from inside the room, "Yes, Esther. I'm coming right away."

17.

In the car, we rode in silence for several blocks. There was nothing appropriate for me to say and I waited for Miss Colby to make her decision. It couldn't have been easy for her, because what she said was, "When you were talking about her husband, you asked, '*Was* he a citizen?'"

"Did I? A slip of the tongue. I was thinking of him as her ex-husband. Is she still in love with him?"

"I have no idea."

After a while she said, "Possibly I made a mistake. There's evidently more to it than I know. I'll pay you, of course, for the time you've put in——"

"I couldn't accept it. It's possible, as I said, the thing will just die. If Turner is behind it——"

"Behind what?"

"You said it was Turner who had been making all the fuss——"

"Yes, I did, didn't I? It was only a guess."

"I haven't told anybody."

Her shrewd eyes were studying me.

"I think I like you," she said. "I just hope you're right in guessing that it will die."

"I hope it will."

"It makes me so damn mad, about the telephone."

"That reminds me, you might expect a visit from the telephone company in your office tomorrow. I reported your phone as in need of service."

"You what?"

"In a casual way, as an old friend. They may send a man out to check."

"You didn't tell them who you were?"

"No."

"All right. I'll go along."

"My guess is they didn't bug your home phone, but maybe they did. I'll take a look, if you wish."

"No, thanks. I'll be circumspect."

I found her street and turned into it. The man in the gray suit was gone and I pulled up behind a two-year-old sedan parked in front of her house.

"Thanks for what you've done," she said. "I hope you understand—it's just that I can't bring myself to say to her, 'Now, my dear, these are the things I believe in—you go out and fight for them.' She doesn't have enough security."

"It's hard to fight for anything without doing it partly for someone else. You're farther out in front than she is."

"Perhaps, but she has more to lose."

We sat there. Pretty soon I said, "Would you like to have dinner somewhere?"

With some reluctance, she said, "Thank you, but

I'm suddenly without appetite and I'm afraid I'd make bad company."

She reached for the door handle and I got out and went around to help her. As we walked toward the porch of her small frame house, I said, "I'm a little curious. I keep wondering how you happened to call me instead of someone else?"

"You have a good, clean reputation."

"Thanks. Anything else?"

"Well," she said, "I'm a sentimental old gal, in a diabolical sort of way. This may sound a little silly, but about ten years ago, my favorite pupil out here was a bright, pretty little girl who had an enormous crush on you. You were in the papers at the time. She fell for you head over heels, the way youngsters do for remote, romantic figures. She even wrote a theme about you. The assignment, as I remember, was to write about some prominent person in the news. Most of them chose politicians, movie stars. But this girl picked you. She did a good job of it. It got under my skin. It was so unusual, I made a copy of it, which I still have. So the other night when I got to thinking about Lorraine Kadek and her problem, I thought about you. That's the sentimental part of it."

I waited and pretty soon she went on.

"I thought Mr. Turner might be behind Mrs. Kadek's problem and I was thinking of him at the same time. The little girl who wrote the theme was his daughter, a beautiful, bright girl named Sherry. Isn't that diabolical?"

"In a way it is," I said. "Have you seen Sherry Turner recently?"

"Not for a long time, but I'll never forget her."

She moved to her door.

"I'd stand here and talk all night," she said. "Thank you for everything. I'm sorry I had to call it off so abruptly."

"If I can help you, give me a ring."

I stopped for dinner at the Lakeside Inn. The food was only half good and I saw no sign of the man in the gray suit. It was about nine-thirty in the evening when I pulled up at Georgiana's house.

18.

The door of her inner office was ajar and I heard her call, "Come in."

She was seated at her desk. The only light was a fluorescent desk lamp and the contrast of light and shadow gave her face an exotic cast. She wore a short, multi-colored smock over a white blouse and she seemed feminine and younger than when I had left her earlier in the day. There was a pile of paper in front of her and she had a pencil in her hand. She looked at me through the lamplight.

"Make yourself comfortable," she said.

"You kept that coffee hot?"

She went to a curtained alcove and came back with a pot of coffee. I sat down near the desk to drink it.

"The license you asked about is registered to a colleague of ours. Beaver Malone."

"I thought he looked familiar. Old Beaver. Wasn't he in the army for a while?"

She nodded. "Intelligence. Wore his uniform around for a couple of years after he was out of the service. Big man!"

"I remember."

Her tone softened. "He's not a bad guy really, just —ambidextrous."

"What have you got on Kadek?"

"A few things. He's one of the best piano players in town. He's an immigrant who has taken out first papers. He goes over big with women. He's about five feet ten inches tall, with blond hair and good teeth; married, with one child, a little girl about four years old. His wife is a school teacher out in the suburbs. He studied music in Europe and Cuba before he came to this country. He's well liked, except he has some woman trouble. They make passes at him and sometimes a husband or boy friend will resent it."

"How the hell did you get all that since noon today?" I asked her.

She shrugged. "On the nightclub circuit I'm pretty hot."

After a while she said quietly, "He's dead, isn't he?"

"Who knows it?"

"I haven't told anybody. Have you?"

"No."

"Nobody who's connected with our great law enforcement organizations?"

"Huh-uh."

She sighed. "Well, you must have reasons. Sometimes I wish I were a man."

"Why?"

"You guys get away with so much murder."

"I wish you wouldn't put it quite that way. I didn't do for him."

"I wouldn't blame you much. She's a pretty little minx."

"Who?"

"Ho-ho-ho-ho. Who!"

"She behaving herself?"

"I don't know. I haven't set eyes on her since she moved in."

"She didn't go out?"

"No."

"How would you know?"

"Please," she said, "I've got the place rigged. Nobody in, nobody out, without ringing a bell."

"You're a good girl," I said, "a good cop and a good coffee brewer. I hand it to you."

"Many thanks," she said. It sounded a little sardonic. "You'd better go talk to your—client?"

I got up and headed for the door that opened on the hall and stairs. I passed close to the desk, and she was squinting at me through cigaret smoke.

"Who beat up on you?" she said.

"Couple of guys. How did you know?"

"A girl can always tell when a man hurts."

"I'll bet that's for sure."

She smiled a little. "Why do you think?"

"You have to have some way to know when to quit."

She stopped smiling. "You'd better go up and see her."

"Doesn't a woman ever hurt?" I asked.

She leaned back some and didn't answer. I noticed for the first time that she had truly feminine contours. She opened her mouth finally to say something and before she could get it out, I leaned over, put my lips on hers and held them there. She stiffened and the chair creaked. Her mouth was cold and stiff, but then gradually it relaxed. She made no other move, not with hands nor body nor head. Only her lips moved slightly and softened and when I straightened, I remembered them as warm. Her eyes held a moment on my face, then drifted away.

"For about thirty seconds," she said, "I didn't hurt anywhere. Does that answer your question?"

"For the time being. Hang around a while. I'll be back."

No light showed under Sherry's door and I hesitated. If she was asleep, it would be good for her to stay that way. On the other hand, I had promised to see her.

I compromised. I tapped so faintly you would almost have had to be wired up to hear it. The last tap had barely died away when she called quietly, "Come in."

I opened the door and looked into a dark room. She fluttered toward me, trailing the nylon negligee. The organdy sleeves crumpled crisply around my neck.

"I thought you'd never come," she whispered.

I held her with one arm, got the door shut and led her across the room. She sat on the edge of the bed. There was a casual chair near it and I sat in it. She leaned toward me, lost her balance and nearly fell. When I didn't move to catch her, she straightened up.

"Everything all right?" I asked.

"I guess so."

Her voice was small.

"Is there anything you need that I can get you?"

"I guess not."

She was punishing me. I tried to roll with it.

"How long will I have to stay here?" she asked.

"I don't know. Aren't you comfortable here?"

"It's not that. It's a nice room. But it's not mine, not like home. It's as if I were in prison."

"Ever been in prison?"

"No."

"It's not like this. It's better than what the city provides for female felons, but it's not anything like this."

"But, Mac, I didn't kill him. I swear I didn't!"

"I'm taking your word for it."

Her tone hardened. "Why did you have to do it this way? Why didn't you just call the police and tell them the truth?"

"I'm not sure what the truth was. I'm not sure now."

"What do you mean by that?"

"Why didn't *you* call the police—and tell them the truth?"

"I was so mixed up——"

"I believe it. Also, no matter what the truth was, you didn't have much of a story. Besides, there were other considerations, weren't there?"

"What other considerations?"

"Maybe you could tell me."

She let that pass.

"You don't have to string along with me," I said. "If you want to bring in an attorney, hire another guy——"

"No, Mac! It's just that I don't know how long I can stand it, being shut up like this."

"Try to think of it as something else. The reason you're here is to give us a little time. Another reason is that when we know where you are, we can move fast, if anything should come up."

There was a pause. When she spoke, her voice had changed again. "By 'we,' I suppose you mean Miss Hennessey and you."

"More or less."

"Is that why you were so long getting here? Were you downstairs with her?"

"For a few minutes."

She turned her head and I saw her eyelashes in profile descend slowly, then rise again. She slumped, putting out a hand to support herself on the bed.

"Sherry," I said, "we'd better have an understanding. I don't want to sound preachy, but I'm about old enough to be your father——"

"No! My father——!"

"The other night you called me for help. When I went to that hotel, it wasn't for sentimental reasons. You hired me."

There was a choking sound from the bed. "Please, don't," she murmured.

"I'm not complaining. It's part of my job to go along with a client. I'm going along now. I'm doing certain things to try and help you and I'll expect to be paid for it, just like a doctor or lawyer."

She kept quiet.

"When the police investigate a death," I said, "they go by the shortest possible route to a definite conclusion. Try to get their picture. You were there alone with him. Your things were there. Your fingerprints were all over the place. You said you'd gone out and come back to find him dead. Who saw you go? Maybe the people in the drugstore would remember, maybe not."

She was lying on the bed now with her face buried in her arms.

"You had opportunity and a motive they could guess at. With the evidence they could see at a glance, plus a little history, they could send you away for the next twenty years. You couldn't plead self-defense. In self-defense, you would have shot him from in front, not in the side of the head."

One of her legs thrashed out and she put her hands over her ears, shaking her head back and forth.

"No," she said thickly, "don't say any more."

"I won't. But you're a big girl now and you have a right to know what you're up against."

After a while she took her hands away from her ears and lay spread-eagled on the bed, quiet and in a way alone.

"I don't know what you had for Kadek," I said, "or what he had for you. I can't make you a speech about love. I'm in favor of it. I think if everybody had a little more of it, coming and going, the world would be in a better condition. I don't know how to bring it about, not for you or anybody else. I'm pretty sure it can't be done by this kind of talking. But maybe this kind of talking can have some other uses. Maybe if I keep it up long enough, I can at least put you to sleep."

She turned slowly onto her side and curled up on the bed, bringing her knees up toward her chin.

"I ran into a friend of yours," I said, "a Miss Catherine Colby."

"Miss Colby? The principal at the school?"

"That's the one. She told me you were a bright, beautiful girl. I like to think of you that way."

"Where did you meet her?"

"It doesn't matter."

"Did she really say that about me?"

"Yes."

"I always liked her. She always seemed to understand."

I got up from the chair. I hurt everywhere inside. I hurt in some new places that nobody had touched from the outside. I thought of Georgiana.

"Maybe you'd rather go to your father's house," I said. "Do you want me to get in touch with him?"

She raised herself wearily, leaning on one hand. "No," she said. "I'm never going back there."

I found a scrap of paper in my pocket and wrote my telephone number on it. I put it beside the phone on the bedside table.

"If you want anything," I said, "if you get scared, for any reason, call me."

"All right."

From the door I looked back at her in the dim light from the street.

"If you admire me," I said, "if once, as Miss Colby

said, you had a 'crush' on me—I feel good about it. It's part of love in a way. If I remember you as bright and beautiful, that's part of love too."

She watched me from the bed.

"Okay that way, Sherry?"

"Okay, Mac."

I went out then and downstairs to the hall. The office door was open and the lamp still burned. But Georgiana was gone. She had cleared her desk except for a large manila envelope. On top of it was a piece of yellow paper with a scrawled message.

"Mac," it read, "pain killers can be habit forming. Here are the notes I made about your problem. I'll stay with it until you call me off. Good night. G."

I picked up the envelope, found a pencil and applied it to the paper below her note.

"Sleep tight," I wrote.

I turned off her light, went out the front door and made sure it was locked, crossed to my car and climbed in. The night was cold and I drove with the windows rolled up.

19.

Georgiana had amassed a pile of background on Kadek. It took me an hour and eight cups of coffee to get through it. She had it well classified and her description of him as a musician would have done credit to any

metropolitan newspaper critic. Apparently it had been
the piano playing that sent the women flipping. There
had been a number of them. Two were his wife Lorraine
and his daughter Trudy. There were half a dozen more.
Sherry Turner was not one of them and there was no
hint that any of the relationships had been initiated by
Kadek or that any of them had developed beyond the
flirtation point.

The names themselves told me nothing. Even if they
had told me a little, I was by no means ready to start
asking questions of a bunch of girls about Kadek. I had
decided to let the police make their own discovery and
investigation and I would have to go through with it. I
could wind up out of business, or worse, if it should go
wrong, but I could make it go wrong for sure by asking
questions of the wrong people.

While I was congratulating myself on having won
this little struggle, I ran across a name I had read, but
failed to notice—a man's name: Bud Phelps.

"Another piano player," Georgiana had written.
"He and Kadek frequently work the same spots, on and
off. They even roomed together for a while. Phelps isn't
the musician Kadek is and doesn't work steady. Works
out of town a lot. He's been somewhere out of town the
last couple of weeks and opens tonight at the Bantam
Club where Kadek closed yesterday. May be some connection between Phelps and Kadek's wife. I got the idea
Kadek had taken her away from him."

I would have to say for her, she had up-to-the-minute
sources of information. The part about Phelps and Kadek's wife could mean something or nothing.

I studied the stuff some more, then locked it up in

the four-drawer filing cabinet and poured another cup of coffee, stoutly laced with brandy. It was eleven-thirty and it would have been a good time to go to bed, except that I kept thinking about this Bud Phelps. It would now be the peak of the evening at the Bantam Club and no time to ask questions. Later, business would fall off.

I got out the big dictionary that I had bought second hand for ten dollars, opened it carefully to keep the loose pages from spilling out and looked up the word *love*. There were three of them: *love, v.t.; love, v.i.,* and *love, n.* Under the noun there were nine definitions, including some kind of flower and no score, as in tennis. The definitions that had to do with the subject at hand weren't much help. Most interesting was the description of a game called "Love," in which "one player, without looking, guesses at the number of fingers held up by another."

That, I thought, might be a way to pass considerable time.

To pass a little immediate time, I crossed the street to Tony's newsrack and picked up the late papers. It was a quiet night and I sat at his bar and read through them and there wasn't a word about Kadek. There was a story, prominently featured, about the citizenship ceremonies coming up the day after next in Federal Court. Thumbnail biographies of some of the big names who were to become citizens were included and the court proceedings were to be followed by a public celebration in Grant Park. A big day for a number of people. Kadek's name wasn't listed, although it would be about his time now. I thought briefly about the guy lying dead in the apartment with the blue walls and the fish around the bathtub, then pulled my mind into other channels, left the papers for Tony and went back to the office.

At one-fifteen I got in the car and drove the few blocks to the Bantam Club, a medium-sized cafe near Rush Street, with a faded canopy over the walk and a sign on the dark doors reading: CLOSED. On a small card I read the name *Sanderson* and a telephone number.

From a sidewalk booth I dialed Sanderson's number and let it ring a long time. When a man finally answered, he made it clear that I had disturbed him. I apologized.

"I'm trying to get in touch with a piano player named Bud Phelps," I said. "I thought he was opening at your place tonight."

"He didn't show. That's why I closed up."

"He sick or something?"

He cussed some. ". . . Can't trust those goddam musicians anyway."

"Do you know where Phelps lives?" I asked him.

"Hell, no."

"I think I'll look him up. Maybe I can get him around for tomorrow night."

"Don't do me any favors," he said and hung up.

Phelps was listed at a nearby exchange. When I dialed it, I got a disconnect reference. I memorized his address and got in the car again.

20

It was an old brick apartment house in the neighborhood of Bughouse Square. It looked dark all around but you can't always tell from the street.

I climbed three flights of stairs and found his place halfway along the bare-walled, carpeted hall. I found it by the sound of piano music, subdued but unmistakably live. There was dim light under the door.

When I knocked quietly, the music stopped and I waited through half a minute of silence. Then the latch clicked, the door opened to the faint clang of the chain bolt and a guy looked out at me through the crack.

"Yes?" he said.

"Phelps?"

"That's right."

"I just talked to Sanderson."

"Who?"

"Sanderson. Bantam Club."

"Oh—well?"

"He said you didn't show up tonight. I wondered if you were sick."

"I'm all right. I didn't feel like working."

"I thought we could talk over a new arrangement."

There was a pause.

"You in the business?" he said.

"In a way."

"What arrangement did you have in mind?"

"To start with, how about something on 'Sweet Lorraine'? She ought to be good for another go."

I waited. Finally the crack closed and I heard the chain drop; the door opened and he was holding it for me.

Unlike Kadek's place, this was a standard, drab flat. The walls were papered, the floor hadn't been waxed for years and the furniture was Grand Rapids *circa* 1930, solid and ugly. There was an upright piano against the wall beside the door.

He was a nice-looking, well-set-up guy, about thirty, with blond hair and big hands. He closed the door, replaced the chain bolt and nodded me to a chair. I sat in it and he sat on the piano bench with his hands on his knees. He didn't take his eyes off me.

"What's with the 'Sweet Lorraine' bit?" he said.

He looked all right to me, not spooky or oversensitive.

"I thought you might talk to me a little about Lorraine," I said.

"Why?"

"She's in some trouble."

"What kind of trouble?"

"You know where she's working?" I said.

He thought it over. "Yes," he said. "Do you?"

I nodded and named the suburb.

"Teaching school," he said.

"That's right."

"You're from the police?"

"No. I'm private. I'm on her side. Hers and Miss Colby's."

"Miss who?"

"Miss Colby. She's the school principal."

He rubbed his hands lightly over his knees and shifted his position on the bench. "Well, if a good kid like her is in trouble—sure. Let's talk it over. You want a drink or something?"

"It might go good."

He left the room and I heard him moving around in the kitchen. When he came back he had a couple of glasses, a bottle of whisky and some ice in a bucket. He set them on the floor where we could both reach them. After I had poured some on the rocks, he bought himself a shot and swallowed it whole.

"I keep trying to forget her," he said. "What kind of trouble is it?"

I was taking a drink and when I didn't answer right away, he went on as if talking to himself. "Man, what a torch I carried for that kid. I mean a *beacon!* I was lit *up!*"

"She's a good-looking girl."

"A real doll. You should have known her before. This chick—man, I can't describe it."

"When you say before, you mean before Kadek?"

His face clouded. He poured himself another drink and downed it. "I guess that's what I mean."

"You've known Lorraine a long time?"

He rubbed his hands over his face. "See, we went to school together, little school down in the state. We were music majors. We went real steady down there. When we got out, Lorraine taught school a while and I came up here—" he made a wry face—"to make my way."

"How's it going?"

He shrugged. "Can't complain. This stuff—like the Bantam Club—is no good. You work a few weeks and the cats want a change. But I got other things. I do a little arranging, write out a few songs. I can make ASCAP in a couple of years."

"After the teaching, then, Lorraine came up here?"

"For a vacation, one summer. She hung around a while."

"And that's when Kadek beat your time?"

He looked away for the first time. "This Kadek," he said slowly, feeling for the words, "he was nowhere."

I guess I was staring at him.

"Excuse the jive talk," he said. "You get in the habit. Kadek—a good musician, I'll say that. He could lay down a Latin beat—well, the hell with it."

He kept talking about Kadek in the past tense, but maybe it was part of the language.

"A good musician," I said. "But as a guy——?"

"As a guy—an ordinary guy—strictly for the women. I guess that's normal. But there was something extra in it, the way they would go for him."

"And Lorraine went for him?"

He seemed to grope again in his mind. "The chick was a soft touch, full of love. That summer she was here, I could have laid her every night and twice on Sundays; only at the same time, I couldn't. Not that I'm so different from other guys, but *she* was different. You couldn't take advantage of the kid."

"But Kadek could, is that it?"

"Kadek was working a joint on Rush Street. I used to take her there and we'd sit around. Well, he would sit there with that big charm——"

He let it drift away.

"Did you put up a fight?" I asked him.

"At the time—I don't know. A thing like that, how can you fight? I liked her. I didn't *own* her. When she told me they'd got married, I was sick, man. Real sick. But I lived. I don't know. You live."

He looked around the room as if it were new to him.

"Then you figure," I said, "it was just this big charm of Kadek's that fascinated her?"

"I don't know. See, Kadek was from Europe. He had to renew his passport, or something, every so often. I guess he thought, if he would marry an American girl, it would be harder for them to throw him out of the country."

"Was he a Communist?"

His face went dead. "What kind of a question is that? I don't know about communism——"

"Forget it," I said, "I don't care. Tell me something; that first summer she came up here, where did she stay? Did she have her own place?"

"No. She lived with her sister."

"Esther Jarvis?"

"Yeah, Esther. 'Dirty Gertie' we called her—behind her back."

I kept quiet. After a minute he said, "It wasn't very nice to call her that. She couldn't help the way she looked. She did a lot for the kid, even after they were married. She worked in some office up here."

"You mean they all lived together after Lorraine married Kadek? Sister and all?"

"Esther kind of took care of her. I think she took too much care of her, but I guess it was a habit with her.

Lorraine couldn't bring herself to tell Esther to get out and leave them alone. Maybe if she had——"

"Kadek didn't go for having the sister around?"

"Well, he wasn't home much. He worked nights and went to school in the day."

"And played around some?"

He looked at me sharply, suddenly unfriendly. "No, he never did."

He looked at the floor, rubbed his knees, then poured another shot.

"I mean," he said, "not that I know of. I tried to tell Lorraine—she worried about the way they went for him. I used to see her sometimes. She'd invite me for dinner. Kadek didn't mind; I always got along with Kadek."

He had seemed to be started on something, but whatever it was, he dropped it.

"She never got reconciled to it—those girls that fell for him?"

He shrugged wearily and rubbed his eyes with his hand. "I don't know. I haven't seen her for a while. After she went away to have the baby——"

"Went away?"

"Yeah, some town downstate. I guess it was cheaper down there, for the hospital and doctor and all."

"Did she go alone?"

"No, Esther went with her, as usual."

"Was Kadek happy about the baby?"

"You couldn't tell about him. He mentioned it a couple of times. You couldn't tell. I ran into him a couple of years later and he told me she'd left him."

"Was he broken up over it?"

"Couldn't tell." He looked at the floor. "I guess he took it pretty hard."

"You didn't try to look her up after that?"

"When a thing is dead, it's dead. By then I had some things going, had another girl. Why would I dig up an old thing like that?"

There was some silence. He started to pour another shot, but changed his mind.

"You said she was in trouble," he said.

"I guess I did."

He got on his feet suddenly.

"Look," he said, "this Kadek isn't a bad guy. No matter what I said about him. Not long ago, I wasn't working much, he even put me up at his place for a while. You talk to him and he'll probably help the kid. He's still her husband."

"I haven't been able to get in touch with Kadek."

"I'll give you his address. He'll be coming home from wherever he's working. He don't hang around much after work."

He moved quickly to a desk, got a pencil and wrote something. When I looked at it, it was Kadek's address all right.

"You talk to him," he said. "He'll help the kid."

I looked at him and he looked back steadily.

"Whatever you say," I said.

He shrugged. "It's up to you, but go see Kadek. He'll help."

"I'll do that."

His eyes strayed and he sighed deeply. "Okay," he said.

As I walked away, I heard him replace the chain.

Even in the sound of the sliding bolt there seemed to be relief.

Lights were burning in the downstairs apartment of Kadek's building and I sat in the car and looked up at the dark windows on the third floor. I had an impulse to laugh, but restrained it. He would have to lie alone a while longer. It wasn't only that those downstairs lights continued to burn. It was also that when I had left with Sherry, I had locked the door, not only against curious friends, but against myself too.

Good for me. I was relieved. The air up there would be getting a little unpleasant. It would continue to get more and more unpleasant hour by hour and the irritability of the discovering police would be increased— retroactive—in proportion.

I shivered in the cold night and drove away fast to my own neighborhood.

Tony had closed up and the street was deserted, except for a cat that scrambled silently across the walk as I climbed toward the street door. Someone had locked it and I had to find my key and it took some time. I got it open and went into the vestibule, heading for my office door, then stopped short to look at the woman who sat on the inside stairs, asleep with her head against the banister rails.

I touched her shoulder and she woke, startled, pulling away. It was Lorraine Kadek. She moved a large purse across her lap, uncovering her other hand, and there was a gun in it.

21

I let go of her shoulder.

"It's all right," I said, "it's me."

I helped her to her feet. She held the gun in one hand and her purse in the other.

"What were you going to do with the gun?" I asked.

"Silly, isn't it?" she said shakily. "I thought I ought to have it——"

"Not so silly."

I slid my hand carefully down to her wrist and she let me take the gun. It was a small automatic, toylike in size, but real enough. I opened it and there were five slugs in it. I couldn't tell by sniffing whether it had been fired recently or whether there had only been five to begin with.

I put it in my pocket and got her into the office, where she brushed at her skirt and started to fix her face. It was a very good face and worth taking care of, but I wished it would come out from behind that wall and get over on my side, if only for a few minutes.

"What brought you?" I asked. "Has something come up?"

"I should think you would know better than I," she said.

"I beg your pardon?"

She leaned forward in her chair and spoke with some

urgency. "I came to ask you, please, not to go any farther with this. I know you're very competent and that Miss Colby was trying to help me. But to go on with it now will do more harm than good."

"That's all right with me, Mrs. Kadek, but would you mind telling me whom it will harm most? yourself, your sister, Esther Jarvis, or your husband—Kadek?"

She gave me a startled blink.

"Or," I asked after a moment, "maybe an old friend, Bud Phelps?"

"What do you know about him?" she said.

"Not much. What's there to know?"

"Nothing," she said. Her fingers were crawling over the strap of her purse. "I don't want to discuss it. I just don't want any more prying and snooping——"

Considering her condition, I had been wrong to probe. But I was in a tight position. I knew too much and at the same time not enough and I couldn't afford to let her build that wall any higher. I got up and moved around the desk.

"I understand how you feel," I said, "but maybe you ought to give some thought to protecting yourself, as well as others."

Her eyes were hostile, confused and pleading all at once.

"You still insist this school board investigation is serious," she said.

"Any investigation is serious to its subject."

"But I've done nothing! They'll learn that. I'll be cleared and they'll drop the whole thing."

"They may drop it, but you won't necessarily be cleared; not unless somebody says so publicly."

She made a helpless gesture. I heard footsteps outside and the door rattling and wondered who among the fellow tenants was coming in so late.

"Somebody forgot his key," I said, "excuse me."

"It's my fault, I'm afraid," she said. "I locked the door."

I nodded and went out to the front door. The knocking resumed as I approached it and I opened it quickly to shut off the racket.

They came in at me, the salesman one step ahead. I tried to sidestep, but the space was narrow and each had a grip on me before the door swung shut.

They walked me to the door fast and inside. Mrs. Kadek was standing in the middle of the room and her eyes opened wide. She clutched at her purse and backed slowly away till she stood against the far wall. The two security men stopped dead when they saw her and the big one found his voice first.

"You might want to leave the room, Mrs. Kadek," he said.

They were holding me high up on the arms, shutting off my circulation. They had good strong hands and I was helpless as a puppy in the bitch's mouth.

"Better go," I said to her.

She stared at me, then straightened against the wall and set her face firmly.

"No," she said.

I had to admire her guts, if not her judgment.

"What's the pitch this time?" I asked them.

"We're looking for Sherry Turner," the salesman said. "You tell us where she is."

"Just put me down," I said.

"Give us the information, Mac. No trouble."

"Nobody squeezes anything out of me."

"We can try," the big one said grimly. "You want to go now, Mrs. Kadek?"

"I don't know you!" she said and it was as if she had spit at them.

The big one put on some pressure, leaning against me as the salesman eased off. I stood jammed against the desk at my sacroiliac, the big one holding me and the salesman around in front now. I could no longer see Mrs. Kadek.

"Don't want to hurt you, Mac," the salesman said. "Where's Sherry Turner?"

"How would I know?"

His mouth twitched. I could see him winding one up, and there was absolutely nothing I would be able to do to stop it or get out of the way. The big one had me in a double hammerlock, bent back over the desk, with my legs pinned at the ankles by one of his own. I wouldn't even be able to kick the son of a bitch.

The salesman had his fist knotted now and his arm cocked.

"One more break," he said. "Where is she?"

I tried to move my left foot, but the big one kicked at my shin hard just as the other pulled it back and started to throw it. I wanted to close my eyes but I didn't dare. I tried to stiffen those muscles he was aiming for, but I was stretched back too far. He could put it clear through me, if he should try.

Then I heard light, sudden steps and a click behind

me. The salesman's punch started out all right, then swerved and glanced off my bottom rib as he ducked away to his right. I felt the big one relax his hold and jerked my left arm free and twisted to get at his neck. I got there all right and pried him loose, but nearly broke my other arm when he tried to hang onto it. I pulled that free and he was coming back at me and I kicked him once, but it was high. He stopped but didn't go down. I could hear scuffling behind me and I was scared for her, but I had to get rid of the big one first. I heard her gasp slightly, then a thud, then a low curse. The big one struck at my face with the heel of his hand and I ducked out, kicked him again, in the shin this time and it slowed him enough that I could get my hand in my pocket.

He didn't see the gun at first, but kept coming and I yelled at him to stop, showing it to him so he couldn't miss. He stopped, skidding a little on the floor. I swung around and the salesman was wrestling with Mrs. Kadek. She had the telephone in one hand and I remember wondering what the hell she planned to do with it, then I saw she was trying to club him with it.

I backed off enough to hold the big one with the gun and barked at the salesman to let go of her. He paid no attention. He got hold of her wrist and twisted till she dropped the phone. She was putting up a good fight, but he was bigger and stronger and they were so tangled up together, I couldn't shoot him.

I told the big one to call him off and gave him another look at the gun. He yelled something, but the other one was having too much fun now. He had both arms around her, holding her against him, and she kicked at his shins, but didn't connect much. She was very red in the face and it was not all from exertion. He was making pretty free with his hands.

The big one watched them with his mouth open. I got the gun pointed where I wanted it and squeezed off. It made an absurd kind of pop, but loud enough. The big guy took a step back, looked down at his leg, very surprised, and slowly took a seat for himself on the floor. I heard a thud and when I looked, the salesman had let go of Lorraine and she was lying on the floor, trying to adjust her skirt, crying a little. I showed the salesman the gun and backed him toward the door.

"Go help your buddy up and out," I said and he moved to do it.

I backed to Lorraine Kadek, helped her up and told her how to get to the bedroom and bath. She stumbled away across the office.

The salesman was supporting the big one now and they got to the door all right.

"Send your boss around," I said, "and we'll discuss the matter."

The salesman looked back at me.

"To avoid embarrassment, don't come with him."

They went out and the street door slammed and I heard them making their way down the steps.

I straightened my clothes, put the gun in my pocket and rubbed my chest for a while. By the time Mrs. Kadek came out of the bedroom, I had the brandy bottle open and a couple of clean glasses.

She had fixed up pretty well. You could see that she

had been crying and her skirt and blouse were wrinkled, but considering her recent history, she was in good shape.

"Shot of brandy?" I asked her.

"Thank you."

I raised my glass.

"Salud, and many thanks. You saved me some pain."

"I didn't do much," she murmured, looking down.

"That's not your line," I said. "You did damn well, lady."

"Who were they?"

"They work for Mr. Roscoe Turner."

"*Our* Mr. Turner? I can't believe it——"

"Well, maybe you'll never have to."

She set down her glass, looking thoughtful.

"But if that's what you've been going through because of me——" she said.

"Please. It seems to me you're carrying enough guilt over your sister and husband. Don't add me to it." I hadn't meant it to be, but when it came out, it sounded brutal. I tried to make up for it. "Also it seems to me," I said, "it must be past your bedtime."

She tried to smile, but it didn't come to much.

"I'll drive you home," I said.

"No, please——"

"I insist."

She came along as far as the door, then pulled back and looked at me with startling frankness.

"The real reason I wanted you to stop this thing," she said, blurting it out, "is because of Karl, my husband. The day after tomorrow he'll become an American citizen. It means a lot to him. I'd never be able to live with myself if I cheated him out of that."

"I understand," I said. "Why did you leave him?"

"Because—I was young and foolish—and didn't know—because I made demands on him no man should have to meet and was hurt when he protested——" she shook her head blindly. "I can't tell you any more."

I let a few seconds pass.

"All right. Can you tell me where you got the gun?"

"The gun?" She registered slowly and didn't ask for it. "It belonged to Karl. When we separated, he gave it to me. I don't know why." She looked at me with a puzzled frown. "I'd forgotten all about it. I ran across it in a bureau drawer the other day. I thought it had been put away somewhere."

"All right," I said again. "Let's get you home."

She came along then and got in the car with me. It had begun to grow light when I swung onto the Drive and started north at a fast early morning clip. Halfway along, she fell asleep with her head against my arm.

22.

At her door, when I lingered, she looked at me questioningly.

"I'd like to pick up that box under your back steps," I said. "Shall I go around by the drive?"

"I'm sorry," she said. "Please come in."

I followed her into the house and the aroma of coffee drifted in from the kitchen. Esther Jarvis was standing in the hall, watching us. She wore a shapeless woolen bathrobe over flannel pajamas. I found it impossible to look at her directly.

"Hello, Esther," Lorraine said.

"I worried about you."

Lorraine gave up trying to smile. "I'm sorry. I had to try and get things straightened out."

Esther turned without a word and went back to the kitchen.

"Excuse me," Lorraine said. "I have to change."

"I hope the day goes well."

"If I can keep my eyes open——"

She climbed the stairs, holding the banister, as if dragging all her weight, step by step.

Well, I thought, she had a rough night.

I headed back toward the service porch. Esther Jarvis was waiting for me in the kitchen doorway. I tried to meet her eyes.

"Cup of coffee?" she said.

I gestured toward the back door.

"Thanks, but I want to get that box and get going——"

"Surely you could use some coffee," she said. "You must have had quite a night—you and my sister."

I looked at her then. "We did some talking," I said.

"Just talk?" she said, with mock surprise. "Judging from my own experience, I can't see you being satisfied with talk."

She turned abruptly and walked away toward the

breakfast nook. I followed. She poured coffee into a cup. She didn't offer it to me and I didn't take it.

"What kind of experience did you have with me, Miss Jarvis?" I asked.

She shrugged, looking away. "Of course," she said, "I don't know what the conditions were. Lorraine is a smart girl, not so easy to maneuver——"

"Maneuver?"

"Yes," she said, "like with the box in the hands —showing me—that intimate contact, leg against leg——"

Then I got it. The smile felt tight on my face.

"Oh," I said, "I see. And then later, worming my way into the house for a cup of coffee—who knows how far it might have gone? But you put up a good fight——"

That bitterness flared in her unhappy face. She spoke through clenched teeth. "Don't make fun of me!" she said. "You might get around me. I don't count. I'm just a housekeeper. But Lorraine is a fine, decent girl——"

Small feet pounded down the hall and Esther broke off, turned away and busied herself at the table. I felt a tug at my pants leg and Trudy was there, looking up, with the pony tails and a clean dress.

"Hi, Mac," she said, "you want some more flowers?"

"That would be nice," I said.

We left the kitchen and I followed Trudy through the service porch into the back yard. I stood there, trying to think of a way to talk to Esther, and Trudy was pulling at my hand.

"The flowers are over there," she said, pointing.

"Suppose you pick some," I said, "while I get the box out."

"What box?"

"You know, the radio box, under the steps."

"You going to take it away?"

"Yes."

"To fix it?"

"Yeah, honey, to fix it."

"Will it make music then?"

She had a hell of a good memory for her age.

"I just don't know," I said. "I'm not sure. I'll see what I can do. How about those flowers?"

"All right."

She flew off across the damp grass. I went down to the driveway, looked under the steps and the box was still there. I crawled under and got hold of it. For some reason, maybe because of the way I had replaced it, or because Trudy had been monkeying with it, it didn't come down easily. I was a little impatient and when I yanked at it, the coiled wire fell and got tangled and it took some time to free it and get it out from under. When I finally got it done, Trudy was standing on the drive with a handful of flowers, watching me. I re-coiled the wire. While I was doing it, she came close and put her arm on my back.

"Won't it work at all?" she said.

She was looking into my face with that look that belongs exclusively to the very young.

"I'll try to make it work," I said.

She held out the flowers and I managed to hold them and the box at the same time, squatting there on the drive. She had her arm across my shoulders and I was reluctant to dislodge it. It occurred to me that maybe I was a little punchy from lack of sleep.

"Are you going away now?" she said.

"For a while."

"Can I come and see you some time?"

"I wish you would."

"Well, how would I know where you live?"

It was a good question.

"Your mother knows where I live."

"But she might not be able to go with me."

I dredged up a smile.

"Tell you what—whenever you want to come and see me, just get in a taxi and tell the man to take you to where Mac lives."

"I know what a taxi is."

"You're a bright, pretty girl."

She looked up suddenly and her face changed. I followed her look and saw Esther Jarvis standing inside the screen, watching us. Trudy's arm slid down over my back and left me. I got on my feet.

"Come in and have your breakfast," Esther said.

"Is 'Raine having breakfast?" Trudy said.

"She'll be right down."

"I'm going to wait for 'Raine!"

Esther disappeared. I started down the drive and Trudy came along, skipping beside me. I couldn't think of anything to say to her. When I got into the car, she clung to the open window.

"Be sure and put the flowers in water," she said.

"I will."

"Good-by, Mac!"

"So long, Trudy. Have fun."

She let go then and backed away. I waved and started off slowly and she ran beside the car for a while. When I turned at the corner, I saw her standing by the fence, still waving.

In front of the office, I put the wired box behind the car seat. My pocket banged heavily against the door jamb and I found I had forgotten to return Mrs. Kadek's gun. I decided maybe this was just as well and locked it in the glove compartment.

Inside, I sat briefly at my desk and watched a single piece of early mail come through the slot and flutter to the floor. I picked it up and it was a postcard, postmarked late the previous night in Milwaukee. On the back, in a sprawling, nearly illegible hand, were the words:

Mac: Better come on fishing. Donovan.

It was nine-thirty in the morning and outside, people were hurrying to work. They would all be late. I took off my clothes, set the alarm for one P.M. and went to bed.

23.

I woke with a thick tongue and a headache. My internal organs felt normal, but the tape on my chest had begun to draw and itch and after breakfast I went to the doctor's office. He cleaned me up and put on a fresh batch of tape. He started talking about X rays and I talked him out of it.

As I was leaving, he said, "You're a real tough guy, huh?"

"Not especially."

"I've been reading up lately. Seems to me, the only motive a man could have for going into your kind of work is an unconscious drive to self-destruction."

"Very interesting."

"But pay no heed to me. I'm only a frustrated butcher."

"Many thanks," I said, and left.

I thought about it, walking back to the office, but not for long. There were other things to think about. I sat in the office, thinking about them, and pretty soon the telephone rang. It was Catherine Colby.

"The telephone man came this morning," she said.

"What did he do?"

"He checked all the instruments, disconnected the one on my desk, took it away and came back with another."

"What did he say?"

"He said he wanted to take it down to the shop and check it."

"That's all?"

"He seemed unhappy. He was scowling a lot."

"I'll bet he was."

There was a pause.

"Mac——" she said, then stopped abruptly.

Faintly I heard a knocking and Miss Colby's voice saying, "Come in," another pause, and, "Lorraine!"

Then absolute silence, as if she had covered the mouth-piece with her hand. I shifted the thing to my other ear and waited. After a moment there was a sharp crack and I guessed she had dropped the phone onto her desk. The line was open again and I heard Lorraine Kadek.

". . . I called Louise Heineman to substitute. She'll be here any moment——"

"But couldn't we talk it over?"

"I'm sorry—I just don't see any way out. Good-by, Miss Colby."

There were footsteps, the slamming of a door. I waited for close to a month, then Miss Colby spoke again, "You heard?"

"Yes," I said. "She resigned?"

"I don't understand—she's overwrought——"

"I'll meet you at her house in an hour," I said.

"Thank you," she said and hung up.

I called Georgiana's number and a woman answered and said Georgiana was out. I asked whether Miss Smith was all right and she said she had gone out too. I left no message.

I looked up Beaver Malone and dialed his number. When he came on he sounded sleepy. I identified myself and he perked up some.

"How's every little thing, Mac?" he said.

"All right. You have a job now, Beaver?"

"Nah."

"You want to meet me around five, down in the Loop? I'll buy you a beer."

"Sure. Fish and Chips?"

"Okay."

I couldn't figure it out about his not having a job. He had had one the day before.

I tried again to get Georgiana, found she was still out and switched the thing over to my answering service. Then I washed up, went to the car and headed again for the North Shore.

Miss Colby sat in her parked car, waiting. I helped her out and we pushed through the gate and went up the walk toward the porch.

There were no dolls having a tea party in the front yard this time. Trudy didn't come running to meet us, carrying flowers. All the shades were drawn, as if the people in the house had gone away on a vacation. When I rang the bell, it echoed inside. After a long wait, we heard quiet, shuffling steps on the other side and the door opened.

Lorraine Kadek looked out at us, nodded and stepped back to let us in. She wore a light-colored housecoat, belted tightly around her slender figure. She had let down her blond hair and removed her makeup. She seemed drained of life, but still moving, with stiff, doll-like gestures.

"Please sit down," she said.

Miss Colby went to a chair and sat down. Her face was distant, abstracted. For the first time since I had met her, she seemed to move like an old woman. She glanced at Lorraine, then averted her eyes hastily, the way you do when you catch someone unwittingly exposed.

Mrs. Kadek had sat down on the arm of an overstuffed chair, leaning against the wing, with both hands folded loosely in her lap. I sat on the edge of a sofa with my hat in my hands, trying to read behind the pale mask of her face.

"We were getting along pretty well," I said. "It seemed to me we had them on the run."

"I'm sure you had," she said dully. "You've been very good—and brave—both of you."

"What I meant was," I said, "there's not much sense putting up a fight if there's nothing more to fight about."

"No," she said, "I guess there wouldn't be much sense in that."

I looked at Miss Colby, who was frowning.

"What is it, Lorraine?" she asked. "Surely you can talk to us——"

Lorraine came to sudden life. She pounded her fist on her extended thigh, then got up and moved quickly around the room, pausing between us.

"There's nothing!" she said. "You can't just be always fighting! Things come up—you can't fight about." She turned suddenly in a swirl of skirt, and held out both hands, begging for understanding. "What do you want me to do?"

"May I have a drink of water?" I asked.

"Of course," she said. "I'll get it."

"I'll get it," I said. "Don't bother. Anybody else?"

There was no answer.

I went to the kitchen, found a glass and filled it at the tap. There were dirty dishes in the sink. It looked as if the kitchen hadn't been straightened since breakfast. I set the empty glass down and went back to the living room. Mrs. Kadek had gone back to the chair arm and Miss Colby was looking at nothing.

"This may not have anything to do with anything," I said, "but what does your sister think about your resigning?"

Her head turned slowly and she looked at me for quite a while. I don't know what she saw or what it meant to her, but pretty soon the dam began to break.

"I don't know," she said. "She's gone."

Miss Colby got up slowly.

"What do you mean, she's gone?"

Mrs. Kadek was staring at her folded hands now and her voice was muffled. "We had a quarrel—at breakfast," she said. "It was silly, the whole thing, but it was violent. She had got the idea—" she looked at me for a moment—"she thought that you and I——"

"All right," I said, "go ahead."

"Anyway, after I got to school, I called her, to straighten things out, and she said, 'I'm going now, Lorraine. Good-by.' Just like that, flat and final. I begged her to wait till afternoon, till I got home. She finally agreed to wait that long. But when I got home, a little after two, she was gone, with all her things."

Miss Colby beat me to the next question. "Where's Trudy?"

"Esther took her."

"You mean that Esther took Trudy and just walked out?" Miss Colby said. "What have you done about it?"

"Nothing. What can I do?"

I had seldom seen a woman so totally defeated. And it didn't fit. I had seen her in a fight and knew she wasn't afraid.

Miss Colby put her arm around the other woman.

"Lorraine, dear," she said, "we didn't know how upset you must be. We won't think of anything else except getting Trudy back to you. We'll call the police, and Mac will help——"

Mrs. Kadek twisted away and her face was no longer blank and dead. "No!" she said. "Not the police! She's my sister! She's been taking care of Trudy—and me too—for years. Maybe she has more right to her than I do. Please, let it go, just let me get straightened out——"

She broke down then, crying, and turned away from both of us. She moved blindly into the center of the room, found she was going in the wrong direction, half turned back and stopped with her face in her hands.

I nodded to Miss Colby and she joined me at the door.

"I'll start a quiet search," I said. "Will you stay with her?"

"Certainly."

"I'll call you."

24.

From somewhere in Evanston I checked in with my answering service. A man named Turner had been trying to reach me every ten minutes for an hour. I called Georgiana, gave her a description of Trudy and Esther

Jarvis and asked her to start a hotel check and to locate Trudy's birth information.

"Is Miss Smith in her room?" I asked.

"Yes. She was gone most of the day."

"How does she seem?"

"Very young and pretty."

"Lay off it."

"What do you want me to do if I find this Jarvis woman?"

"Just sit tight."

"You're full of that, aren't you?" she said. "Yesterday it was 'sleep tight,' now it's 'sit tight'—by the way, what does it mean?"

"If I didn't know better," I said, "I'd think you were trying to woo me in your womanly way."

"God forbid."

"That's my girl. See you later."

As I hung up, I wondered briefly whether Georgiana might become a problem. Then I decided probably not. More likely I was my own problem and aren't we all?

The Fish and Chips went well with Beaver Malone's personality. It was noisy and crowded, but you could talk in there without attracting attention.

Beaver came in a few minutes after five, found me in a rear booth and squeezed his thick frame in across from me. He looked a little like the back of a catcher's mitt with the guy's hand in it.

"Things kind of slow?" I asked.

"I was working up to this morning. Good job."

"You close it?"

He poured his beer expertly.

"I lost it. Shame, too. It was a cinch, a lead pipe."

Another thing about Beaver, he was full of original expressions.

"That doesn't sound like the old Beaver Malone," I said. "How could you lose it?"

He made a bad face. "I don't understand it. I don't know *how* they got onto me."

I decided not to tell him.

"What I've got," I said, "won't get you rich, but you might make a few bucks."

"Sure, Mac, if I can help——"

"It involves some bugging."

"It's tricky. Big risk in it."

"I know. This job is out in the suburbs. I'll see you get portal to portal pay. I only want the bug in an out-building, a detached house behind the main house."

He nodded and poured the rest of his beer.

"You want it for radio pickup? How close?"

"Not close. It would have to carry."

All of a sudden he was staring into his beer. When he saw that I noticed, he went ahead and took a drink.

"You say a house in the rear? What is it, a mansion or something?"

"More or less. Fellow named Turner—Roscoe Turner."

I was watching his knuckles. I thought for a minute he was going to break the glass in his fist.

"Once again, Mac, what was that name?"

"Roscoe Turner."

He turned his head slowly and looked out into the joint. "I can't take the job," he said.

"But you need a job, Beaver, and I need you."

"Can't do it," he said. "Thanks for the beer."

He got on his feet and started away. I put my hand on his arm.

"Wait, don't make me just sit here," I said. "If you can't take on the job——"

But Beaver couldn't wait. I finished my beer, left the place and drove back to the office.

Turner was waiting for me, pacing restlessly in the hall. I opened the door, nodded him in and showed him to a chair. He took off an expensive-looking hat and placed it carefully on a corner of my desk. I couldn't read his face any better than I could that first night.

"I'll come right to the point," he said, sitting erect with his immaculate hands on his knees. "Where is my daughter?"

"If you're referring to a girl named Sherry," I said, "whom I have met briefly, I assume she's capable of getting in touch with you, if she should want to."

He colored and I knew he could be hurt.

"I feel sure," he said, "you know where she is. It's important to both of us that I see her. I would appreciate your co-operation."

"I'm sure of that."

"You don't choose to tell me?"

"If I know where she is, I don't choose. If I don't know, there's no choice."

He was no dim-brained, pompous shell. He was a negotiator and politician. He sat calmly in the chair for about a minute, then got on his feet, walked to the window and stood looking out with his hands locked behind his back. He made a good standard picture of distinction.

"I can understand why you feel vengeful toward me," he said. "But I can't understand, in light of the public knowledge I have about you, why you would extend this feud to include an innocent young girl——"

"She is evidently innocent," I said, "whatever that means. But she is not a young girl. She is legally an adult woman and I bear her no ill will."

He turned from the window and gave me the old straightforward appeal. "Then you can't object to telling me this: if she should wish to get in touch with me, is she free to do it?"

I smiled at him, unable to think of a ready answer. The telephone bell saved me. He reassumed his stance at the window as I lifted the instrument and spoke.

"Georgiana," she said. Her voice dropped a notch. "The cops found Kadek."

"I see."

"I just heard it on the radio."

"Yes, go ahead."

"Is there anything I should do? Call an attorney?"

"I would think not."

"Anything else?"

"I don't think of anything."

"Just sit tight, huh?"

"That sounds like a good idea."

"Brother," she said and hung up.

I put the phone down and looked at Turner.

"If I could find your daughter," I said, "and make an appointment for you——"

His composure cracked and he moved toward the desk.

"An appointment! There's no need to be insulting——"

"I might undertake it," I went on, "in return for a small favor from you. Take about fifteen minutes of your time, given an efficient stenographer."

He waited and I let him. Finally he said, "Yes, well——?"

"I want you to write a letter to the Board of Education in your town, with copies for the local papers and Miss Catherine Colby, saying that you mistakenly launched an investigation of a teacher named Lorraine Kadek concerning her fitness for a position in your district; that you now recognize your mistake, have called off the investigation and apologize to Mrs. Kadek for any inconvenience or embarrassment you may have caused her."

His nostrils dilated as he hung onto himself. "No derogatory information about Mrs. Kadek has been discovered," he said. "As far as I'm concerned, she may keep her position for as long as she renders competent service."

"Are we being honest now, Mr. Turner—even as this world goes?"

His color went through some changes, including an interesting lavender.

"I'm aware of your interference in the matter of Mrs. Kadek—and Miss Colby's," he said. "I don't know what fantastic interpretation the two of you have put on it, but there are others like you—muddle-heads, do-gooders—who scream every time a few simple questions are put——"

"Oh, please," I said, getting up. "This never made sense, even when it was spoken by someone who pretended to believe it. You went after Lorraine Kadek hoping you could drive her back to her husband and get your little girl off the hook with Kadek. You didn't even have the reasonable motive of trying to perpetuate yourself in office."

He went into a kind of slow, undulating convulsion, gradually straightened himself out, picked up his hat and set it carefully on his head.

"I had a higher opinion of you," he said. "I took you for a man of the world. I find just another mush-mind, a bleeding heart——"

"Yeah," I said, opening the door for him. "Well, God help me when my heart stops bleeding."

I don't know that he heard me. I held the door while he went out, pushed it shut and went to the telephone. I dialed the operator and got Mrs. Kadek's number. Miss Colby answered.

"How is she?" I asked.

"She's feeling better. Have you found the child?"

"No. We ought to have help, the police——"

"She won't hear of it."

"All right. This is important. In the papers pretty soon and on the radio right now, they say Kadek is dead, her husband, that is. Sooner or later there will be police out there to talk to her."

I waited through the silence.

"Yes?" she said.

"Can you get her to go to your place?"

"I think so."

"I have to leave it to you."

"Yes, all right. Please call as soon as you find Trudy."

"By all means."

I hung up. "By all means," I had said. By what means? I didn't even know the make of the car, or whether she had the car. I didn't know what the luggage looked like. I thought about how long it takes a real good skip tracer to run down a desperate, unimaginative deadbeat, and then I quit thinking about it because it was making me sick. Another thing that was making me sick was hunger in the stomach.

I don't have time to eat, I thought. Then I thought, If you don't eat, it won't matter whether you have time or not.

I left the office, crossed the street, picked the latest papers off Tony's newsrack, went inside and ordered a quick sandwich. The sky and my stomach were getting dark.

The paper contained no mention of Kadek, but it was an afternoon edition and the late issues wouldn't be around for another half hour. I chewed my way through the sandwich. The joint was noisy and confused and I escaped into the telephone booth in the rear and dialed my answering service. When the girl came on, she sounded hysterical, like everything around me.

"I'm glad you called! I was afraid——"

"Slow and easy," I said. "What's the trouble?"

"There were some policemen here, about forty-five minutes ago. They wanted to know what calls you had today——"

I became aware that the earpiece of the instrument was pressing too hard against my skull, and had to think out consciously the mechanics of easing it off.

"They got me so confused! I'm sorry—I didn't——"

"You mean you gave them a list of my calls."

"I—yes."

"Including the calls from Georgiana Hennessey?"

I heard small choking sounds.

"You never have to give them that information," I said. "They didn't have a leg to stand on."

"I know, but they——"

She started to cry. I could hear the sound of it like distant waves.

"All right," I said, "don't worry over it. If they come back, or if this ever happens again, remember, you don't have to give them information like that. They won't hurt you. They might try to scare you, but they won't touch you."

She managed to say, "Thank you for being so nice about it——"

"I don't have any more time now. Just don't tell anybody anything."

"I won't."

"So long, kid."

I hung up and left the joint and ran to my car. It was a long way to the South Side, but it was not a bad traffic time and with luck I could make it in half an hour.

I made it in twenty-eight minutes. My watch read seven-forty-two.

A squad car was pulling away as I approached and I gave it time to get around the corner before climbing out. Then I went fast up the walk and into Georgiana's waiting room.

Her office door stood open and I saw her standing beside the desk. She had a whisky bottle in one hand and was pouring from it into a water glass. It was all she could do to hold it. She paid no attention to the tinkling bell nor to my footsteps. I went in slowly, watching her. She set the bottle down on the desk and, holding the glass in both hands, took a long drink. Her face was the color of raw cauliflower. I waited till she decided to look at me and when she did, I wished she hadn't.

"Just in time," she said.

"Did they pound on you?"

She shook her head. "No." She reached for the glass, changed her mind and dropped her hand so that it lay strangely on the desk, limp and useless. "They just talked to me."

I waited.

"Sticks and stones . . ." she said, "like hell."

She decided to take another drink and I waited some more.

"I'm not oversensitive," she said slowly. "I'm a lady cop. I've handled lady lushes, lady killers and ladies of the streets. I've heard all those words from all kinds of mouths. I know exactly what they all mean. But I never heard them before like I just now heard them from those two—hyenas!"

It was an anticlimax, but she had evidently heard the vocabulary exhausted and could never hope to top it. She sat rigid at her desk, gripping it with both hands, and after a minute or two she began to cry silently and all that moved was the tears on her face and the muscles in her throat.

I walked around till I found a glass, poured myself a slug of whisky and drank part of it. It tasted like kerosene. I went to the kitchen and ran some water in it, but it didn't help. I poured it down the sink.

Back in the office, I found her telephone directory, looked up a number and dialed it. She sat there. The tears had stopped, but now and then her throat moved convulsively.

The phone rang at the other end, six, seven, eight times. Finally a man answered.

"Larry?" I said. I told him who I was. "Would you like to walk down to the corner drugstore and let me pick you up in about half an hour?"

"I've got a couple of things, Mac——"

I waited and pretty soon he said, "It's that hot, huh? Okay, half an hour."

Georgiana was looking at me.

"What are you going to do?" she asked.

"That was Larry Fisher. I'm going to turn her in."

"For her sake?" she asked, "or mine?"

"Let's not get mixed up. For everybody's sake and in the interest of law and order."

She was coming back together again.

"It's your case," she said, "but the kid is pretty young."

"True, but Larry Fisher isn't."

"He can't work miracles."

I looked at her with sudden curiosity.

"When did you get filled in on the details?"

"The two snakes," she said, "to soften me up. They said Kadek had been shot by some woman who shared his apartment. They got onto you because a couple of night crawlers saw you in front of Kadek's place from their prowl car. They worked on your answering service——"

"I know."

"So they put two and two together and started to cherchez la femme. They damn near got away with it."

"What did you tell them?"

"Nothing. They wanted to search the place and I went legal on them. I said not without a paper and if they persisted, I could have a lawyer in the house in five minutes. And I could too."

"That scared them off?"

"You don't scare them. You just confuse them. They were upset. Kadek had been dead for almost three days when they found him. They didn't like that and they didn't like it that they didn't know who they were looking for. They can stand anything except to look bad in front of each other, and they would have looked bad if they had rounded up all the women in my house and tried to make a decision on one of them."

"Who were they?"

"O'Connell and Robinson."

We heard the light footsteps outside the hall door at the same time. I reached it first and, looking up from the bottom of the stairs, saw the flat soles of ballet shoes running away along the upstairs hall.

"I'll go talk to her," I said. "Will you call Larry Fisher and tell him to make it an extra fifteen minutes?"

"Mac—take it easy with her."

"Gentle as a down puff," I promised.

She didn't run to meet me this time. She was sitting in an armchair with her knees crossed and she seemed quite calm. Her breast rose and fell a little more rapidly than you would have expected, unless you had seen her running up the stairs.

"Still feeling caged?" I asked.

She shrugged lightly. "I feel fine."

"No bad dreams last night?"

"Not even good ones. I just slept."

"Good for you."

I pulled up a straight chair and sat down. "I have to talk to you a little," I said, "and some of it may be frightening. But it won't be as bad as it may sound."

"Go ahead," she said. "I'm a big girl now."

"The police have found his body and have already been here looking for you. Georgiana sent them away. She took quite a beating doing it."

"I'm sorry," she said formally.

I went a little formal myself. The hell with her.

"I've decided it's time for you to turn yourself in voluntarily, so the police can check out your story and clear you."

She cocked her head in a birdlike gesture. "Voluntarily?" she said.

"Of course. I'm not going to drag you down there. But I'd hate to see the cops come and drag you down there. Things will go a lot more smoothly if you go in now and tell them your story—all of it."

There had been time for it to catch up with her and I watched her stop breathing for a moment, then resume unevenly.

"What will they do to me?" she said. "Will they shave my head? will they make me put on one of those— uniforms? will they lock me in a cell with some prostitute?" She was breaking up like dry cheese. "Not that I'm any better than one," she said.

"Take it easy," I said. "They won't shave your head. A good lawyer will go with you, to the District Attorney's office. A man will ask you to make a full statement. You may have to do a lot of sitting around, waiting, but nobody will touch you, if you don't scream or fight."

"What will happen next?"

"You'll go through a formality—you'll be what they call 'booked'—either as a suspect or as a material witness, more likely the latter, since we're rushing them. The lawyer will arrange to have bail set, you'll meet the bail through another formality, and they'll let you go."

"And what if they book me as a suspect?"

I decided there was no sense holding out on her. As we had both said, she was a big girl now.

"Then it may not be possible to arrange bail. They may hold you for a few days, not for long. And they won't shave your head; nobody will hurt you."

She did something vague with her hands and found a place for them on the arms of the chair. "You have it all arranged?" she said.

"I'm meeting the lawyer in a few minutes."

"What if I don't want to do it that way?"

"I can't force you to do it," I said. "But if you stay here, the men who talked to Georgiana will be back and after that, things won't go quite the way I've described them."

She said nothing.

"Your father came to see me today," I said. "He wants to get in touch with you. I didn't tell him where you are, but if you want to go home to him, I'll take you."

She thought it over—or something.

"I don't want to go home," she said finally.

"Then I'll go get the lawyer."

Downstairs, Georgiana was seated at her desk and she looked all right, though she had been alone long enough to get scared.

"If they come back and start to sound off," I said, "you might dial operator and leave the phone off the hook. They won't keep it up long."

"That's real timely advice."

"I just now thought of it. You're a good girl, Georgiana. I think I could love you."

"Not tonight, Napoleon. Anything to do about Miss Smith?"

"No. We talked it over. She was a little snotty but she went along all right."

"Anything else?"

"If you feel up to it, just keep looking for Esther Jarvis and the little girl. They have to be found and I can't think of anybody to help with it that I can trust. If you locate them and can't reach me, call Miss Catherine Colby, out north. She's in the book."

She followed me to the door.

"Mac—" she said softly, "some time—not tonight, but some time——"

I squeezed her hand. "When I can get up my nerve," I said.

She smiled and it was her old smile, half warm, half mocking, and I was glad to see it.

26.

Somewhere in Jackson Park, I sat in the car with Larry Fisher and told him the story—nearly all of it. He listened without interrupting and when I finished, he sat looking out the windshield, not moving, just thinking. He was a wise man, and tough, and it felt good just to be with him.

After a while he said, "How'd you ever get yourself tangled up like that? You've been around long enough to know better."

"It seemed to me she was in no condition to go through the mill at the time. Also she's holding out, even on me, and I like to think she has honorable reasons."

"How come you didn't call Donovan?"

"Donovan's gone fishing, up north."

"Great. You plan to go in with her?"

"Only if you say so. I can't afford your fees."

"What about her fees?"

"Her old man is loaded. American Electronics."

He nodded. "You think he might have done for the boy himself?"

"Or his flunkies—I've thought about it."

"Any other leads?"

"A couple of ideas."

"You better get started, boy. I think this girl is in trouble." He looked at his watch. "I'll have to make a deal. I hope the right guy is in."

We drove back to the drugstore where I had picked him up and went to a phone booth. Larry dialed a number and we waited. He was a wiry, taut guy, with a lined, leathery face. He didn't smile much. He dug a cigaret out of a battered package and I lit it for him and leaned against the open door of the booth. We had to wait quite a while because the right guy was not in and he finally had to settle for an assistant D.A. named Kutnink.

"Yeah, Kutnink, Larry Fisher talking," he said. "I think I can bring you the girl you're looking for in that homicide—Kadek—?"

He listened briefly.

"No," he said, "I can't do that. I'll bring her in myself to your office. She'll give you a statement. Then we'll see."

The voice on the other end rose sharply and Larry held the receiver out from his ear and shook his head at me sadly. When he spoke again, his voice was casual, even bored. "I wouldn't worry about it, Kutnink," he said. "He was shot in the right temple, wasn't he? Simple enough. He got word they were going to deport him and he didn't want to go back to Czechoslovakia. So he shot himself. Wouldn't you?"

He glanced at me deadpan. I could only marvel. When he got into action he was like a smooth running machine that never ran out of oil.

"Look," he was saying, "you're not talking to the Rotary Club now. What do you mean they wouldn't send him back? They sent a couple back to China not long ago. You know that . . . Check with the Immigration people; you'll probably find the whole answer right there."

He waited some more while Kutnink sounded off. An inaudible sigh was the only sign of impatience he showed during the conversation. The sound of sputtering on the other end faded and Larry said, "All right, we'll be in. I'll be honest with you. I think maybe she's a material witness; that's all. I'll expect her release on her own recognizance, or bail if we have to. She's a responsible citizen. No reporters, Kutnink. We'll just get in and out quietly."

He listened again and the next time he spoke, it was with quiet, definite finality. "Those are the terms. If you have to stall, you can call my answering service. I'll wait to hear from you."

He came out of the booth, digging for a new cigaret.

"I guess it's set up," he said. "Let's go get the girl."

We drove to Georgiana's office. On the way I said, "I never thought about that deportation angle. Maybe he did shoot himself."

"It's possible."

A little later he said, "It'll keep 'em busy for a while anyway. The Immigration people don't know their ass from a hole in the ground these days."

At Georgiana's, Larry called his answering service and told the girl where to reach him. He lit a cigaret, looked at us in turn and shook his head.

"I don't know how you people stay in business," he said.

"We got a special talent," Georgiana said.

"Let's talk to the girl," he said.

I headed for the hall door. A faint buzzer sounded and Georgiana let out a yelp. When I looked around, a light was flashing on a panel in one corner of her desk.

"The back door," she said.

I heard them come along behind me as I got the door open and found my way along the hall toward the back. The kitchen door was swinging gently. I pushed through it and the back door was wide open. I opened the screen and saw her running along the rear walk toward the high fence that bordered the alley. She was carrying her bag and she didn't set it down at the gate, but jerked at the latch and got through it. I started down the steps, calling her, but Larry put his hand on my arm.

"Let her go," he said. "I can't force her to go down

with me. If I had to do that, it would be a shambles."

"She's a fugitive——!" I argued.

"She's been a fugitive for two, three days."

Georgiana's telephone was ringing and when we got into the office, she held the instrument toward Larry.

"Yeah?" he said. ". . . yeah, honey, thanks." He hung up. "Kutnink," he said. "He says all right to bring her in; no reporters, no cops." He pushed his hat back on his head, pulled the phone over and dialed. I heard him say, "Kutnink? Larry Fisher. I guess you missed the boat. The girl's gone——"

He held the instrument away from his ear and Georgiana covered both of hers with her hands.

"Cool off, Kutnink," Larry said. "You had to take time. You can't always have time. I never said I had the girl locked up. You gave her time to spook and run. . . . Sure she's a fugitive. Good hunting."

His cigaret had burned to his fingers and he dropped it into an ash tray.

"I'm sorry," I said.

"Forget it. I was busy."

I offered to drive him home and he waved me off. "I need the exercise," he said. "So long, Mac. Good night, Gorgeous George."

After he'd left Georgiana said, "You want a drink?"

"No, thanks."

"The little girl was born in Danville on April twenty-third, nineteen fifty-one: full term baby, to Mrs. Lorraine Kadek. The kid almost didn't live through it. She had an RH blood factor and they gave her transfusions like crazy. She pulled through."

"You're a good girl."

Her steps sounded strangely light crossing the room. She held out a paper and I took it and stuffed it in my pocket. She remained close to me.

"I'm not so good," she said, "but maybe I'm this good. I wouldn't run out on you."

I couldn't say anything. I don't know what she read in my eyes—depletion? weariness? or the memory of Sherry Turner running away down this or that alley? Whatever it was, she moved away suddenly, as if I had slapped her.

"What are you waiting for?" she said hoarsely, "the Queen of England, to throw herself at your head?"

"No. If it helps any, I thought of it before you mentioned it."

"Many goddam thanks!"

I tried to tell her. "It's just that I've got this thing all loused up now and I have to straighten it out——"

I went to the telephone directory on her desk and dug into it. There were a hell of a lot of Turners, but only one Sherry, living on a side street off the old Gold Coast: thirty minutes' drive.

I headed for the door and she let me have it, full voice, yelling across the room with her back to me.

"I hope you find her! Just don't ever tell me about it!"

"I hope I do, too," I said, "because she owes both of us quite a lot of money and I won't be left on the hook for it."

I waited a minute, but she didn't say anything and I went out. It was a bad way to leave, but it was the only way I had at the time.

27

There was a fog that thickened as I drove north toward the Gold Coast and I pushed through it doggedly, cursing it with whatever remained in the back of my throat.

I found her address on one of those dark, quiet streets of old homes converted to apartments, with two or three modern buildings to each block. I drove past it, stopped on the opposite side of the street and got out of the car. Then I got back in again abruptly. I had caught sight of the security patrol, the two of them, as they turned to retrace their beat along the walk in front of her building.

I wonder how much it costs Turner, I thought, to operate that private goon squad.

The big one was limping, but not badly.

Well, I thought, he has big legs and it was a small bullet and medical science is wonderful.

Headlights swung into the street behind me and I adjusted the mirror. Mr. Turner's black sedan pulled in to the curb on the wrong side and came to a jolting stop in front of the building. A rear door opened and Turner got out and walked rapidly to the door. Behind him walked another man, carrying a brief case.

I wonder whether he's as good as Larry Fisher, I thought. And then I thought, No, not in that world.

I started the car and pulled away. Clearly, she had

run home, called Papa and Papa had come with an
attorney to get everything straightened out and no
doubt he had sent the two bully boys ahead. All of which
had been sound strategy because, assuredly, undenia-
bly, I had shown up.

Good luck, Sherry. . . .

To avoid the traffic jam at my corner, I went on for
three blocks to make the left turn off Michigan, turn-
ing back into the dead-end street that ran out at Tony's
corner and which, if continued, would cut off half my
office across the way. I was more than a block short of
the street's end when I saw the squad car in front of the
office. I turned in to the curb and switched off the lights.
I could see them sitting there, two of them, in the front
seat.

I wondered whether they were thinking up some more
bad words.

Sticks and stones, Georgiana had said.

Believe you me. Not only sticks and stones, but anything else that might come readily to hand.

I got out, walked slowly to the alley behind Tony's
and went through his back door and kitchen into the
joint. Business was good, but it was all at the bar and
the room was relatively peaceful. I went into the phone
booth and got Miss Colby's number. I could feel the
strain behind her voice when she answered.

"I'm going to be tied up for a while," I said to her,
"and I think you ought to call the police and start
them looking."

"Lorraine just won't have it."

"Family loyalties can be carried too far."

"I don't know. I just don't know."

"I have someone working on it. If she finds them, she's to call you."

"All right." Her voice lowered. "I haven't told her yet about—you know. I was hoping to have some good news first."

"I'm afraid there's no good news. I saw Turner, but he wouldn't budge."

When she spoke again her voice broke, then she got hold of herself and firmed up. "I'm sorry, Mac, I got you into such a mess."

"Getting in and out of messes," I said, "is part of my life. Things work out."

Do they not? I thought.

"Is there any way I can help?"

"Just take care of yourself—and Mrs. Kadek. Those kids will be in school tomorrow, mostly on time."

"So they will."

"Good night, ma'am."

I left the booth and sat down at one of the rear tables. Paula stepped away from the bar with a drink on her tray and brought it to me. I went to work on it slowly, enjoying a simple pleasure.

I enjoyed it fully, and when it was gone I sat for some time staring at the empty glass. After a while I walked to the front of the joint and Tony nodded good night from behind his cash register. I went outside, took a couple of deep breaths and crossed the street toward the office.

As I stepped up on the opposite curb, the doors of the squad car opened and three men got out, two from the front and one from the rear.

28

They came along with me up the steps and into the hall. Two of them were the detectives, O'Connell and Robinson, whom I had seen around for years. The third was a younger, scrawny man wearing rimless glasses on an official face. When I stuck my key in the lock, he pulled something out of his pocket and said, "So that everything should be legal, this is a paper authorizing us to search your premises. Do you want to read it?"

I glanced at the paper.

"Nice of you to go to all that trouble," I said.

He put it away and I unlocked the door. As I opened it, O'Connell, the bigger of the two cops, stepped in front of me.

"I'll go first," he said, "then you. Then the others."

I stepped out of his way. He pushed on in and groped for the wall switch beside the door. I blinked against the sudden light as we walked in and the guy with the glasses pushed the door to and leaned against it.

O'Connell went to the desk and began pawing through the things on it. In Donovan's absence, this man would be in charge of homicide and it provided him with a certain incentive. He would never get to be in permanent charge of homicide because his lack of imagination was almost total and because he didn't know how to get along with anybody, even other cops. He was a beefy one and I had seen him beat a crucial murder witness so thoroughly that when they brought him into court, the judge declared him incompetent and wouldn't take the testimony and the D.A. lost the case. The witness, the last I heard, is still in some mental hospital.

Apparently nothing on top of the desk caught his fancy and he started opening drawers, pulling stuff out. Some of it fell on the floor and he let it lie there. He didn't look at much of it, just yanked it out and threw it on the desk or the floor. There wasn't much of importance, mostly paper. After a couple of minutes, the other one, Robinson, went to help him.

I didn't know Robinson too well. He was the brooding type. I had heard that he was an ace marksman, could shoot from any angle, fast and under any circumstances and could nearly always hit what he aimed at.

I stood there, watching them strip my desk drawers. When they finished with that, O'Connell headed for my filing cabinet.

"Everything in there is confidential," I said. "Your paper doesn't include that because no officer would include that on a warrant."

O'Connell looked at Four-eyes, who took off his glasses and put them back on. His face made me think of lemon juice.

"You have a license to operate as a private detective?" he said.

"You must know I have."

"May I see it?"

Oh, Christ, I thought and got out my wallet. When

I offered it, he shook his head. "Just take out the license," he said.

I took the license out and handed it to him. He didn't read it. He tore it into pieces and dropped them on the floor.

"Does your paper cover that?" I asked him.

He didn't bother to look at me. "On my own responsibility," he said, "as an administrative officer. Go ahead, O'Connell."

O'Connell rattled the file.

"If you give him the key," Four-eyes said, "it won't be necessary to damage the cabinet."

"If he's big enough," I said, "let him get his own key."

O'Connell started toward me across the room. He was big enough and he could do it all right, with the help he had, but he would come out of it with some awfully sore equipment.

Four-eyes stopped him. "Go ahead, break it," he said.

O'Connell probed at the lock with something, but it didn't work and he wasn't the patient type. Robinson moved to help him and they pulled the cabinet out from the wall and pushed it over onto the floor with the drawer handles up. Robinson climbed onto it and held it down while O'Connell yanked at the bottom drawer till it came out. All I had in it were old telephone directories. He threw them and the drawer out of his way.

They straightened the file up and Robinson reached in through the bottom and tripped the lock. O'Connell started through the drawers, starting at the top. He would pull out a folder and glance at it and when he saw it wasn't what he wanted, he would throw it on the floor. Paper began piling up around his feet. When it bothered him, he would kick it aside.

In the middle of the third drawer, he found what he wanted, pulled out a folder and showed it to Four-eyes.

"This is it," he said. "Says *Kadek* on it."

"I'll take it," Four-eyes said.

Robinson brought it to him and he stuck it under his arm.

They lost interest in the files. O'Connell went to the bedroom door, twisted the knob and kicked it open. I thought about how it must look in there. Nobody had straightened it much since Sherry had used it and there would be lipstick stains, one thing and another.

O'Connell disappeared and I heard him plodding around. Pretty soon he stuck his head out the door and looked at Four-eyes.

"There's been some dame in here," he said.

He glanced at me without expression.

"It was your mother," I said.

He started for me, but Four-eyes stopped him again. "Hurry it up," Four-eyes said. "We've got to get back."

O'Connell looked at me some more, then returned to the bedroom. I tried to think of a way to get him so hot that Four-eyes wouldn't be able to stop him, but I couldn't think of it. He didn't have enough imagination.

When he came out, Four-eyes asked, "Nothing else?"

O'Connell shook his head.

"Let's go," Four-eyes said.

O'Connell pulled a set of handcuffs out of his pocket. This might be the time, I thought.

But Robinson had imagination. As O'Connell came forward and I set myself, Robinson moved in behind and grabbed my shirt collar, twisting it. I gagged and tried to back into him. O'Connell kicked my legs out from under me and I fell on my left side, banging my head on the floor. Robinson put his knee in my back. They got my hands back there and O'Connell snapped on his manacles, squeezing them tighter than necessary. When he jerked on them I felt the skin tearing on my wrists, but the ringing in my head was more uncomfortable.

"Get on your feet," O'Connell said.

Four-eyes opened the door. O'Connell gave me a push and I followed the D.A.'s man outside and down the steps.

"Where's your car?" O'Connell said.

"Down the street."

"Where down the street?"

"You want me to point to it?"

He reached behind me and gave a jerk on the cuffs.

"Walk to it," he said.

I stepped off the curb and we all walked across the street and down past Tony's to the car. It was locked. O'Connell found a brick in the gutter, raised it and threw it hard at the front window. The window broke. He got his hand through the hole and opened the door. Leaning into the car, he looked over his shoulder at Robinson.

"Get the keys out of his pocket," he said.

Robinson dug into my pants pocket.

"Wrong place," I said. "I didn't know you were that way."

"Be easy on yourself," he said between his teeth.

He found the keys in my coat pocket and tossed them to O'Connell and we stood around, waiting. O'Connell unlocked the glove compartment, looked in, then twisted to look out again.

"This might be it," he said.

He reached in with a handkerchief and came out with the gun. Four-eyes took it and put it in his pocket. O'Connell kicked the door shut and some of the broken window fell out.

We walked back to the squad car and I climbed into the back seat after Four-eyes. Robinson got in next and slammed the door. O'Connell did the driving.

They let me ride that way downtown, sitting on the edge of the seat because of the handcuffs. It was a rough ride. When O'Connell would stop suddenly, I would bang my head against the top of the front seat. Nobody tried to help me.

29.

I had never seen these offices. They were high up and off the street. The elevator was small and lumbering and smelled of sweat and faintly of blood. My head had cleared, but my wrists were raw and the strain of having my hands linked behind my back had worked on my chest till my ribs felt freshly broken.

I walked among them down a long, empty corridor, wondering where we were going, but hesitant to ask.

There are always reasons for avoiding the front entrance to the D.A.'s offices; reporters, among others, and all the trappings of due process.

Four-eyes opened a door with a frosted panel and we followed him into a small, bare office without windows. There was a typewriter desk covered with scars and scratches. There was one straight chair against the wall. Beyond the desk was another frosted glass door and light showed through it. I could hear voices faintly.

Four-eyes nodded at Robinson and the two of them went into the next office, leaving me with O'Connell. He waited till the door had swung to, then turned to me slowly, put his beefy hand under my chin, squeezed my face with his fingers and spoke to my nose in a thick voice.

"I got a lifetime grudge against you and everybody like you. You spend all your time thinking up ways to make policemen look silly."

I would have spit in his face, but the way he was holding me, I couldn't have done it without biting myself.

"If you want to play sweethearts with Donovan, that's up to him," he went on. "But I think we got you this time, and Donovan ain't here."

The latch clicked and he let go of me as Robinson came back.

"Take the cuffs off him," Robinson said.

"Oh, no!"

"Take 'em off."

"He's afraid to," I said.

O'Connell's arm went up beside my head and Robinson eased him aside.

"Lay off," he said. "You know who's in there. Take the cuffs off."

O'Connell got out his key, grumbling. He took his time over it and Robinson had to rush him to get it done. When my hands dropped free, blood stabbed painfully in my wrists and fingers. I flexed them to ease the shock and O'Connell snickered.

I would have slugged him then, if I had had any feeling in my hands, but I didn't want to do it when they were numb. If I couldn't feel it myself, I couldn't be sure he would.

Robinson jerked his head at me and I followed him into the next office. This was spacious, with a rug on the floor, a massive mahogany desk and, on a stand beside it, a recorder, warmed up and ready to go with a roll of tape in place.

There were armchairs along the wall to the right of the desk and another under the window behind the desk. Four-eyes was sitting in one of the chairs by the wall. A vacant chair sat facing the desk in the middle of the room. Robinson led me to it and walked over to sit down beside Four-eyes. O'Connell followed him.

In the chair under the window sat a guy wearing a medium-priced hat, a conservative suit and an expression of neutrality. He looked federal.

The man at the desk was heavy set, dressed in a tweed suit, horn-rimmed glasses and a white shirt with a black bow tie. Eventually he nodded and I took it to mean I could sit down, which I did, rubbing my wrists. He didn't seem to notice. When he spoke, his voice had a dry, rustling tone, like gravel running down a tin slide.

"My name is Osborne. I'm a special prosecutor attached to the District Attorney's office. I want to ask you some questions."

I didn't answer, but I guess he hadn't expected any. He went on in his dry, gravelly voice. "I advise you of your right under the law to refuse to answer any question on the ground that it may tend to incriminate you. But I also advise you to co-operate in your own interest. Is that clear?"

He beamed at me.

"It's clear enough. It's not exactly the way I've heard it before."

He went on blandly. "If you come to trial," he said, "you will have the right to your own counsel, the right to cross-examine witnesses, a jury—the usual rights of which I'm sure you are aware."

"I sure am—or was."

He frowned a little and stuck his white hand out over the recorder. "It will facilitate matters and provide you with an accurate record of your own testimony," he said, "if you will permit us to record your answers. Do I have that permission?"

"On one condition," I said.

He seemed confused. "What is that?"

"If I can make a brief preliminary statement."

He glanced at Four-eyes, started to look over his shoulder at the federal man behind him, changed his mind and looked at his wrist watch.

"It will have to be brief," he said.

I stood up.

"You don't need to stand," he said.

"I think I will. Aren't you going to turn on your machine?"

He hesitated, then reached down and flipped the switch. The tape began to rustle across the gadget and rewind itself on the opposite spool.

"I don't understand why these officers came," I said. "I have committed no crime, with the possible exception of a misdemeanor. They found evidence that a woman had been in my bedroom. I confess to this."

I paused, flexing my fingers.

"The truth is," I said, "I had just been entertained by a woman who has been soliciting in our neighborhood for several years. No man is made of wood entirely and I finally succumbed to this woman's charms, partly from desire and partly from pity. She is an older woman, the unfortunate mother of one of your own officers, a Detective O'Connell. That may have been——"

I had started to turn and when he came charging at me across the office, I was ready. Nobody could stop him this time. The distance was too short. He came with both hands out in front of him, making a sound that should have been a roar, but came out more like a loud bleat.

I waited till he was three feet away, swung my foot free, gave it a start from behind and kicked him with it very hard and very low. Then I got it back on the floor and hit him in the face twice, first with one fist, then the other. I could feel it fine, clear to my teeth.

The next moment I felt myself slammed back into the chair and Robinson had his hand in my shirt collar, twisting it as before. It was a good hold. O'Connell was on the floor, holding his groin. His mouth was open and his eyes crooked. Four-eyes was on his feet and so was the special prosecutor at the desk. The federal man looked less neutral, but he hadn't moved.

O'Connell worked his mouth, trying to speak, but vomited instead. Robinson had my head back at the end of my stretched-out neck and when O'Connell let go, I glanced up at his face. It had a disgusted look on it. When he saw me looking at him, he wiped it off and tightened his grip on my collar.

"Better let up," I said, "or I'll do the same thing."

He let up a little.

O'Connell rolled over and tried to get on his knees, then collapsed, face down with his head in his arms. Four-eyes looked at Robinson.

"Better call the infirmary," he said.

Robinson took his hand out of my collar. I straightened it and myself in the chair. The man at the desk was wiping his glasses with a clean handkerchief. The federal man behind him had turned in his chair and was looking out through the blind.

O'Connell let out a squeaky groan and tried to roll over and Four-eyes told him to lie still. I decided O'Connell would be out of my hair for the night, maybe for a week or two.

Osborne had his glasses on again.

"If you think that little demonstration will help your chances," he said dully, "you are badly mistaken."

"It never occurred to me," I said, "that I had any chance to begin with."

He opened a folder on his desk and thumbed in it.

"Why were you hounding Kadek and his wife?" he said.

I looked at the recorder, still running, hearing the faint whisper of plastic ribbon.

"You better get on with it," I said. "You'll run out of tape."

"You refuse to answer?"

"I can't answer it. There's no way."

The door opened and two guys in uniform came to where O'Connell was lying on the floor. They had a stretcher and they set it down and rolled him onto it slowly. O'Connell did some groaning. When they lifted him, he opened his eyes and looked at me. I couldn't hear what he mouthed, but it was easy to read his lips. I looked away from him. They carried him out and a man in a white coat came in with a bucket and some rags and began cleaning up the rug.

"I'm waiting," Osborne said.

I was tired of his voice and the look of him with the big glasses. "Next question," I said.

He made a face. The tape ran out on the recorder and the loose end of it whipped round and round. Osborne switched it off.

"I realize," I said, "you are trying to look good for this guy, who is probably some federal officer. Maybe you could get to be a government investigator. I wish I could help you. But I don't even know what you're talking about."

The federal man leaned forward with his arms on his thighs and looked at the floor. Robinson had got up and was pacing the floor near me. I wasn't afraid of him, but then he wasn't afraid of me either, so we were even.

Osborne jerked something out of his file and I heard paper tearing.

"I will read portions of a statement taken an hour ago," he said, "which I trust will clarify the situation for you."

He cleared his throat and read flatly, in a dry monotone:

> I was a friend of Karl Kadek's. On Friday night, May 14, I was at the White Hall, where Karl was playing piano with the hotel orchestra. That was the night I learned I was being followed by a certain private detective known as "Mac." I don't know his real name.
>
> QUESTION: How did you learn this?
>
> ANSWER: He came there—to the hotel. He wanted information about Karl. I wouldn't give it to him. He said he would stay there until I did, if it took all night. I was frightened of him and left the table. I sent a note back with the waiter, telling him to meet me at the rear exit. Then I left the hotel by another door.

Osborne paused to clear his throat and it was the only sound in the world.

> QUESTION: Where did you go?
>
> ANSWER: I went to Karl's apartment and waited for him. I thought he ought to know he was being investigated . . .

It went on from there, about how she had stayed with him for three days because she was afraid to go home, and of course nothing intimate happened between them; how I (Mac) came there and got in a quarrel with Kadek, threatened him with deportation; how he sent her out for some cigarets and when she got back, Kadek was bleeding on the floor and she moved him onto the bed and just when she was about to call the police, I (Mac) returned and took her away, to a "safe place," so the police wouldn't think she had killed him.

> QUESTION: Where did he take you?
> ANSWER: To some big house—I had a room of my own. I called myself Miss Smith.
> QUESTION: Who owned the house?
> ANSWER: I don't know.
> QUESTION: You don't know where it was?
> ANSWER: No.

After that it got better, about how I had come to turn her over to the police, after promising to keep her from harm; how she didn't trust me, figured the lawyer I promised her would turn out to be some shyster who might make her say the wrong things, whereas she had always been willing to tell the police everything—the whole truth, which, of course, was what she was doing now.

> QUESTION: Go on, please. What happened next?
> ANSWER: Mac went to get a lawyer. When he was gone I packed my bag and went out the back way and went to my own apartment on the North Side.
> QUESTION: What did you do then?
> ANSWER: I called my father and told him I was in trouble. He came with an attorney and I told them the whole story. The attorney had it written down and I signed it.

QUESTION: And this statement represents the whole truth of everything that occurred in the matter of you and Karl Kadek between May 14 and May 19?

ANSWER: To the best of my memory.

Osborne paused. There was no sound. After a minute he said, "Transcribed for Arthur Salisbury, Attorney-at-law, by Ethel Vann, Stenographer. Signed by Miss Sherry Turner, eleven-forty-eight P.M., May 19."

I was looking at the tag end of the tape where it hung out of the spool on the recorder. I wondered whether, for the rest of my life, every time I should see or hear her name, I would get that deep ache in my chest and that gray feeling in the head. When Osborne spoke again I had to fight to hear the words.

"Have you anything you wish to say?" he asked.

I just sat there. Pretty soon he said, "Take him away."

Then Robinson was standing beside my chair, reaching for me. I got up and went out with him. Somebody coughed lightly and there was the sound of the door latching itself behind me.

30.

The long night thudded on, like gobs of mud falling at irregular intervals from a skip-loader. They couldn't get around to locking me up. It was a matter of intense regret to me. In jail I could at least have tried to get some sleep. Instead, I got conversation that never quite made sense. Once in a while I could pick out a name that sounded familiar or a pattern of action that might have happened all right, except that it had happened to someone else, not to me.

They spent quite a lot of time reading to me. They had a deposition from an officer of the Suburban Telephone Company. The guy that read it was only half literate and it took him a while. The gist of it was that I had bugged some telephones and later maneuvered the company into pulling my chestnuts out of the fire. After he had managed to read all the words in it, he said, "Now why would a wise eye like you do a thing like that? You know you can't go around tappin' wires. Even a policeman can't do that without a special order."

He read a statement by Beaver Malone, about how I had tried to hire him to do some bugging out in that neighborhood, but Beaver wouldn't touch a thing like that. The elocution expert heaved a sigh.

"I never figured Beaver was smarter than you."

That was the worst of the interrogation from beginning to end—nothing connected with anything else. I would almost get things lined up in my mind and suddenly they would be on something entirely different. They even got into a discussion about where O'Connell's mother lived. As far as I knew, O'Connell had never had a mother, but I didn't say it; O'Connell was not around. I could still feel him once in a while in my ankle and on the backs of my hands.

I couldn't feel anything else except thirst. All the

rooms were overheated and most of the men in them were smoking. My tongue began to swell in my mouth.

Sometimes they would leave me alone for a while. I would sit and try to drop off in my chair, but the chair would never be big enough to hold me and I would wake with a jerk when I started falling off it. After a while, a couple of them would come and get me and lead me to some other room, where we would pick up with something new.

"Why didn't you inform the Immigration Bureau if you were suspicious of Kadek?"

"I wasn't suspicious of Kadek. I didn't even————"

"Or were you working for his wife? hounding him for money?"

I gave up. There was no point trying to talk to them. Somebody had stuck hot rods up all of them and the word had gone out to get me and tie this thing up tight. It had probably been Kutnink, on account of the deal with Larry Fisher, although Larry had kept my name out of it. Of course, they had already tied Georgiana and me together on it so they could have drawn that conclusion, and it would be safer to take it out on me than on Larry.

I was a little surprised that nobody leaned on me. It wasn't until four-thirty in the morning that I discovered at least one of the reasons: they had better.

They were moving me for the twenty-fourth time from one office to another. My mouth and throat had got so dry that when I tried to say something, the words sounded like the growl of a sick dog. I couldn't even understand them myself.

In the corridor stood a drinking fountain, white and

gleaming against the drab wall. It was a long corridor and I could see the fountain at the far end, during the walk between the two bulls. I could see water spouting up out of it, could practically feel it on my face and in my mouth.

Our destination was a door at the end of the hall, just beyond the fountain. We had nearly reached it when one of my guides mumbled something and stepped aside. He leaned over the fountain and took a long drink for himself. When he finished and came back, the other walked over and did the same. I watched him. The water splashed against his face and he let some of it dribble back into the bowl. I ran my tongue over the dry roof of my mouth.

When he turned back, he glanced past me at the other one and then each took one of my arms and led me on into the new place.

It was a big room, with desks and filing cabinets and a big overhead light in a white metal reflector. They sat me in a chair under it. Half a dozen guys were draped around on the desks, in shadow.

In a corner stood a water cooler on a metal stand. A package of paper cups hung on the wall beside it. During the next period of questioning it was in almost constant use by everyone but me.

The guy in charge was a stranger to me. He was in shirtsleeves. He had hairy arms and a scar across his face and he hit the water jug more often than anybody else. He would shoot out a couple of questions, then walk to the cooler, hold a cup under the tap and drink. Then he would come back and shoot some more questions.

He'd been at it for some time when the door opened and a messenger came in with a manila envelope. Scarface opened it and took out a couple of 8 x 10 photographs and a sheet of paper. He tossed them on the desk and went to get himself another drink. I couldn't watch him.

He came back, picking up the photographs on the way. He held one up in front of me and I blinked at it in the white light.

"This is a picture of a .25 automatic," he intoned. "Detective O'Connell found it in the glove compartment of your car. The fingerprint men say your prints are on it."

He held up the other one.

"This is a picture of two .25 slugs. One of them came out of Kadek's head. The other was fired from the gun in the other picture. They match up."

He tossed the photos on the desk and got himself a drink. Then he came back and stood in front of me.

"Does that seem to you to represent a material piece of evidence?" he said.

I tried twice before I could push the words out of my parched throat. "It's a humdinger," I said.

"Maybe you can explain it to us."

I worked my mouth, but couldn't get anything out. Outside I heard heavy footsteps approaching in the corridor and in a thrust of panic, wondered whether they had got O'Connell back on his feet.

One of the cops slid down from a desk and said, "Poor bastard's dried up. Give him a drink."

"Sure," Scarface said. "Want a drink?"

I sat still. The one who had come down from the desk

pulled out a fresh cup, brought it to me empty and slapped my shoulder.

"Go ahead, Mac. Help yourself."

I climbed out of the chair and made it across the room in silence to the water jug. I held the cup under the tap and pushed on it. Nothing happened—a few dribbles. I shook the jug lightly, then roughly, then caught myself in time and gave up. There hadn't been any water in it. Those drinks they'd drawn for themselves had been dummies. It was an old trick and I might have remembered it.

I went back and sat down. The solicitous one said, "You mean it's empty? That's tough. I didn't know."

Another one said, "Guy'll be around with a new one —about ten o'clock."

I sat in the chair and waited for them to get on or give up. The door opened behind me and there was some stirring in the room. It banged shut and there were heavy steps and the squeak of a chair. One of them said, "Hello, Lieutenant."

Others murmured. Nobody answered, but I could guess. Surely there was no law against guessing.

Scarface, looking over my head, nodded and said, "You want to take over, Lieutenant?"

"No," a voice said gruffly. "Go ahead."

I had guessed right for once. It was Donovan. All I could truly expect from his presence was that maybe a little sense would creep into the conversation. As for the rest of it, he would be in a sour mood because he had either got called back from his fishing trip or had come back voluntarily when he heard about Kadek. Still, the sound of his voice had given me a shot in the arm and I managed to ask an intelligent question of my own.

"Who was the gun registered to?"

"A good question," Scarface said. "Let us take a look."

He took a long look, longer than necessary. Long before he turned back to me, I knew the answer would be no good.

"To Kadek," he said. "It was Kadek's own gun."

I sat there, waiting.

"Well—" Scarface said, "go ahead with the explanation."

Somebody was tapping on a desk with a pencil. I couldn't see him in the shadow beyond the light ring. Somebody coughed. I heard footsteps, the door opening, the gurgle of the water fountain in the hall. Somebody slapped at a mosquito and swore softly.

"All right," I said, "for a drink of water, I'll talk. I killed him. For the most stupid reason of all—jealousy."

Scarface stood still in front of me. There was no more coughing or shuffling or slapping, only the sound of my own cracked voice.

"He was beating my time with this girl. I went to his place. The Turner girl was there too. She told the truth, but not all of it; she was trying to help me. Kadek started smooching my girl right in front of me. I broke it up and sent her out. We got in a big scene. He had this gun right out on a table. Miss Turner ran in the other room and he started after her. I shot him on the run. I put the gun in my pocket and picked up my girl and took her home. Then I went back to Kadek's and the rest of it is the way Miss Turner told it."

I looked up at Scarface. There was no sound.

"I hope you can keep my girl's name out of it. She's had her share of hard knocks. I called her a girl—she's an older woman really—Detective O'Connell's mother ——"

I stopped again because I was too dry to talk. The room was absolutely silent for about thirty seconds. Then I heard the legs of a chair slam quietly against the floor. Scarface had his tongue between his teeth and he took a couple of steps, reached down and grabbed the front of my coat. He pulled up on it till I was no longer actually sitting on the chair.

"Wise," he said between his teeth. "A smart-mouth private eye."

He pushed me back in the chair, but held onto my coat, talking into my face.

"You were thirsty, huh? Man, you're going to be so thirsty, your smart tongue will stick out through your cheeks. I will personally see to it——"

Another chair banged. The gruff voice spoke behind me. "You guys better have a break. I'll take over."

Gradually Scarface let go of me, clinging to me only with his eyes, backed to the desk and picked up his coat. There was a scraping of feet and chairs. They straggled out of the room. The door opened and banged a couple of times and I heard them going away down the corridor. I sat still in the chair. After two or three minutes of silence, I heard a light switch and the light over my head went out. A lamp was burning on Scarface's desk, but for a little while, the room seemed dark as the inside of a glove. I blinked my eyes, trying to start some tears. I thought if they would run down my face, I could catch a couple of them with my tongue.

31.

Donovan walked heavily to the desk, folded his arms on it and lowered his head to wipe sweat off his forehead. When he looked up, his face in the lamplight looked like the face of George Washington on a blown-up dollar bill wrapped around a basketball.

"What am I goin' to do with you?" he said plaintively.

All I could get out was a dull croak.

"You want a drink of water?"

I shrugged.

He came around the desk and I followed him to the corridor. He leaned against the open door while I drank from the fountain. When I'd swallowed enough of it, I splashed some over my face and wiped it with my handkerchief.

"Thanks," I said, returning past him.

"I didn't do it for charity," he grumbled. "I got to have it so you can talk."

"What do you want me to talk about?"

"Set down somewhere," he said.

I found a swivel chair at one of the desks and sat in it, leaning back. It felt pretty good. Donovan sat on the edge of the desk and stared at me for a while. When he spoke, he stressed each word separately, like a boy reading from a primer.

"When you find a dead body you are sup-posed to call the po-lice."

I let it go.

"If you have made that body dead by your own hand, you ain't likely to make the call. But a smart cop like you should know it would be better to make the call, even if you went somewhere else to do it."

I let that pass too.

"That's why the boys here got upset," he said.

"That's not the only reason. What else is behind this big push?"

"I don't know. I just got off the plane."

"I'm sorry about your fishing trip."

"Yeah. You must of had some reason for deceasing this Kadek fellow. You tell me what it was and we'll pick it up from there."

"Did you read through that file they worked up?"

"I did. It made sad readin'."

"Did it make sense to you?"

"Nothin' ever makes sense all the way." He picked up the two photos and waved them at me. "But this makes sense! And you didn't deny none of it. And don't try to tell me you was framed by O'Connell, because he ain't got the sense to work a frame-up. Somewhere he would louse it up."

He threw the pictures down.

"You shouldn't of banged him up like that," he said more quietly. "One thing O'Connell does real good— he holds a grudge."

"Good for him."

"All right! You're real tough. You're tough enough not to worry about O'Connell. But you ain't tougher than me and you know it. And another thing, you ain't any tougher or smarter or lily-white than this police department. Don't forget it."

"I'll remember it."

"They got you in a hole up to your eyebrows," he said. "They have practically got your grave dug right under your feet. Don't that mean nothin' to you?"

"Sure."

"I'd hate to see all that time I spent tryin' to teach you somethin' go to waste. I'm willing to waste a little time right now to save some of that other."

"What do you want me to say?"

"Why did Kadek die?"

I looked at him. I looked through the half dark room toward the lightening window blinds.

"Could I have one more drink of water?"

"Hurry it up."

He went with me again while I got myself a drink. Then he followed me back inside and stood around, waiting. He was pretty good at waiting. I paced around some.

"Why does anybody die?" I said after a while. "A twenty-five-year-old woman shot her father-in-law to death in an argument over an onion. A fifty-year-old spinster in a fancy suburb came downstairs and shot her mother, her bachelor brother and herself without a word. A gray-haired mail clerk killed his wife and wounded his daughter because they laughed at him."

I looked at Donovan, but got no help.

"So why did they die? Not for an onion—not for a

laugh—not because they looked funny in the face."

His face was like a stone. He scratched the back of his neck.

"All right, son," he said, "who did Kadek laugh at?"

I found a chair and sat in it.

"I could guess," I said, "but I can't tell you."

He took off his hat, pounded it into a new shape and put it on again. He came to where I was sitting and he had one hand way out to the side, as if he might let one go at me. He might have, too.

"What do you mean, you can't tell me?" he shouted. "You goin' to sit on your stubborn can in Joliet for the next twenty years because you made some kind of a deal——"

"No," I said. "I'm not going to Joliet for twenty minutes. Because when it comes to a trial and I get a chance to cross-examine the only two witnesses they've got against me, the judge is going to throw the case in the lake and he will let the prosecuting attorney do the tossing."

He looked at me with his mouth open.

"If they let it get that far," I said, "which I don't think they will, because it would be too embarrassing to everybody, including the State Department, the Bureau of Immigration and the Republican National Committee."

He still couldn't get his mouth working.

"And I can name some more," I said, "if you have the time. There's a guy named Roscoe Turner, the Suburban Telephone Company——"

He finally made it. "Will you shut up!"

"You ask me to talk and now you tell me to shut up."

He calmed down some. "All right. You say you got

this big beautiful case. Why not give me a break and let me in on it?"

"I don't think so. I think I'll sit in your goddam jail and let you sweat it out. I've got nothing to lose. They took away my license. I'll let the county feed me."

He was pretty sore now, as I was, and he ground his teeth a little, but when he spoke, he had hit that plaintive tone again. "Why all of a sudden do you take an attitude like this?" he said.

"Because I'm fed up. I haven't had any sleep or any food. I haven't had any contact with any intelligent people and I've been yelled at for the last six hours by one guy and another. I'm sick of being yelled at, especially by you."

"What was that about your license?" he said.

"Some fart-face from the D.A.'s office tore it up."

"That don't mean nothin'."

"It was insulting. I'm sensitive."

"I give up on you."

"Well, it's been a stimulating conversation."

"Too bad we didn't make a record of it."

"I'm sure somebody did."

"What?"

"The whole joint is wired, isn't it?"

"How would I know?"

"I understand that's the way you're working now. The only contacts you guys have any more are with electronic engineers."

There was no reason in the world for him to put up with any of this. I decided he was as tired as he seemed.

"You better take it up with the commissioners," he said. "I got nothin' to do with that part of it."

"Don't give me that. If you boys had your way, you'd have every home, office and institution in the city wired right into a big central switchboard, so you could listen in any time you wanted to. You wouldn't even have to put on your shoes in the morning——"

"Ah shut up. You wanted to set in jail—I can arrange it."

He headed for a telephone. The door opened and a messenger came in. He was a skinny youngster in an ill-fitting suit. He didn't have any chin.

"Lieutenant Donovan?" he said.

"Yeah."

The kid handed him an envelope. Donovan turned it over in his hand a couple of times, then looked at the messenger. "What you waitin' for?" he said.

The kid shrugged and turned away. "Nothing, Lieutenant," he said.

Donovan waited till he had gone out, then opened the envelope and pulled out a slip of yellow paper. He squinted at it, crumpled it and threw it in the wastebasket.

"Come on," he said.

"I get to lie down on one of your fleabags now?"

"No. They want you upstairs. Some guy named Osborne."

"Oh, you'll like him."

"Let's go," he said.

I followed his wide, thick frame out of the room.

Nothing had changed in Osborne's office except his suit. He wore the white shirt and black bow tie and I couldn't tell whether he had changed them or not. I sat in one of the chairs by the wall and Donovan sank with a groan into the next one as Osborne cleared his throat. When he talked his voice was hoarse and he seemed somewhat depressed.

"You would be Lieutenant Donovan," he said.

"Yes, sir."

"We've never had the pleasure. I'm Osborne, special prosecutor. You have a distinguished record."

"Yeah, sir," Donovan muttered. "If it's all the same to you, we'd better get on with it. The prisoner ain't had anything to eat this morning."

"I'm sure he appreciates your solicitude, Lieutenant."

"It's the law," Donovan said stubbornly. "We got to feed them a certain time."

"I see." He pawed through some papers. "There are two gentlemen who wish to speak to the—prisoner." He turned to me. "I may say, you will certainly not prejudice your case by co-operating with them."

Osborne opened a door and two men came in past him. One was Roscoe Turner. The other had a brief case and I guessed he would be that attorney, Salisbury. He looked prosperous, like Turner, but puffy about the face and a little sleepy. But I couldn't hold that against him. He had worked hard the night before, writing fiction.

"If we could have a few minutes alone———?" he said.

Osborne bustled obediently to the door, looking back at Donovan, who blinked in surprise.

"If it's all right," I said, "I'd like the Lieutenant to stay. I have no secrets from him."

Osborne, leaving, looked puzzled, and that fit, and Turner and Salisbury frowned. Donovan regarded me with suspicion. When Salisbury nodded us to the desk for a close huddle, Donovan slid down in his chair and pushed his hat over his eyes. He wouldn't miss anything.

Salisbury spoke briskly but confidentially as Turner leaned close to listen. "I think we can help you," he said.

"I'd appreciate it," I said, "but how much do you cost?"

"I'm glad to do it as a service to Mr. Turner."

"In return for what?"

He frowned and tapped his brief case nervously. "Naturally," he said, "we don't think you killed Kadek. Miss Turner's account, while factually correct, wasn't complete. She told all she knew. As far as your part in it is concerned, there is nothing but inference and conjecture. It's up to the police to solve it."

"All of it?" I asked.

He frowned some more. "I know," he said, "you were under the impression that Mr. Turner had ordered the wholly illegal wiretapping in the surveillance of Mrs. Kadek. But it was done without his knowledge and against his strongest wishes. We know who was responsible and we need the equipment you found at the Kadek house in order to establish the facts and to remove a cloud of unjustified suspicion hanging over Mr. Turner. I'm sure you believe in that kind of simple justice."

I looked at Turner, who smiled stiffly.

"We've had our differences," he said. "Possibly there

was good and bad on both sides. I'm ready to forgive and forget."

"I'm glad to hear you say it," I said. "It couldn't have been easy. But the only thing I want from you I told you about yesterday."

He moved his hands. "That's out of the question," he said. "You're a man of the world, you can understand——"

"I'm not sure I can. Mr. Salisbury here mentioned simple justice. I think that's what I'm talking about."

Salisbury snapped a strap on his brief case and looked gloomy. "I hate to see you make things unpleasant for yourself," he said.

"Well," I said, "I don't see how they could be any more unpleasant than they have been the last few hours."

They got up and stood around.

"That's your final decision?" Salisbury said.

"Thanks for trying," I said. "Maybe you honestly believe that it's more important for a community leader like Mr. Turner to get out from under a cloud of suspicion than for an ill-paid school teacher to get simple justice. If it were just a difference of opinion, we might work it out your way. But it's more than that and I'm stuck with it. I have clients too."

They moved unwillingly to the door. I waited till Salisbury got his hand on the knob.

"There's one deal we might make——" I said.

I watched them freeze, hopeful, but uncommitted.

"I want your file on Mrs. Kadek. In return for that—all of it—I'll hand over all the equipment I found."

Turner didn't like it. I saw the starch work on his

face. But Salisbury had a job to do. "As the file no longer has any value——" he said, questioning Turner with his eyes.

I found a pencil stub in my pocket and the back of an old envelope. I wrote on it the location of my car and the words "behind the seat," and handed it to Salisbury.

"I'm not really trusting you very far," I said. "I have enough evidence without that equipment. But if you'll leave the file when you take the other, I may never have to use it."

Salisbury stuck the envelope in his pocket and they went out. I couldn't read anything in their faces, but faces I never could read. As I rejoined Donovan, Osborne came bustling back into the office.

"I just thought of something," I said to Donovan. "Since I haven't been booked for anything, I guess you won't have to feed me. I'm saving the city thirty, forty cents."

Donovan looked at Osborne. "Ain't he been booked?" he said.

"No, Lieutenant."

Donovan sighed. "Well, it's up to you," he said. "We can book him and feed him and put him in custody, or we can set around here till we all starve to death."

Osborne jerked oddly in his chair and the telephone rang.

"Yes? Osborne," he said. . . . "Yes, he's here now. I'll tell him . . . Yes."

He hung up and looked at me. "You'll leave the room," he said.

"Sure," I said, heading for the door.

"You know what happens if you let him walk out there alone?" Donovan said. "He won't come back, even if you call him."

Osborne spluttered.

"He's a prisoner," Donovan said. "You tell him to go and me to stay—he goes. I can't do nothin'."

"Wait!" Osborne shouted. "Come back here."

I sat down again. Donovan was leaning forward in his chair, looking at Osborne with curiosity.

"If it ain't too urgent," he said, "I'll take him down to breakfast and get him booked and locked up and all, and maybe we could have lunch together—if you ain't tied up."

Osborne learned how to talk again. "That will do," he said. "Mr. Kutnink wants you in his office at nine o'clock."

"You goin' up there too?"

Osborne choked. "It seems to be out of my hands."

Donovan looked at me, got on his feet and nodded. I followed him outside and down the hall and as we got into the elevator, he said, "You know what I'm probably doin' on account of you?"

"Don't tell me," I said. "And it takes a pretty big sling for yours, doesn't it?"

After a minute, he said, "Some day, you and I will go over to Evans' gym and work out for a while—as long as you can stand it."

I didn't say anything. There was no sense in deliberately hurting his feelings.

32

Donovan sent out for coffee and we drank it in the waiting room outside Kutnink's office. It was more pleasant here than anywhere I had been during the night—quiet, with a deep carpet and comfortable leather chairs. There was no secretary. She would be on the other side of his office, serving half a dozen assistants like him. There were only the chairs and a sofa and a small writing table and the cold morning light seeping through the blinds.

We had sat there for ten minutes when the office door opened and Kutnink looked out at us. He was in his shirtsleeves. His collar was wrinkled and his face gray from lack of sleep. He wasn't a big man, but he was thickly built and gave an impression of great strength.

"Come on in," he said.

"Both of us?" Donovan said.

"That's right."

He held the door and we went past him into a large office with furniture identical to that in the waiting room. The federal man was sitting behind the desk, exactly as in Osborne's office eight, nine hours before. There was a bunch of paper scattered over Kutnink's desk. He sat down at it, lit a cigaret and rubbed his eyes roughly.

"Sit down, Lieutenant," he said dully.

Donovan continued to stand, along with me. "If it's all the same to you," he said stubbornly.

The reason behind his attitude soaked in gradually as I remembered out of both hearsay and experience, the bitter, permanent feud between Donovan's branch of the law enforcement system and Kutnink's. I remembered cops sitting around cooling their tired heels and when you would ask, "Where's that one they picked up last night over on the West Side?" someone would say, "He's up with the lawyers," and the brooding silence that would follow. There was plenty to be said on both sides and sometimes Donovan's side would have the advantage, sometimes Kutnink's. But the feud never stopped. God help us all if it ever does.

Kutnink understood all right. His voice was quiet, but the tension behind it was obvious as the almost audible groan of a piano string when the tuner pulls it up. "I hear you decided to take over the Kadek case," Kutnink said.

Donovan spoke flatly without tone. "I was up north. I got a telegram. I come in the place there and some of the boys are running an interrogation. Far as I know, I'm in charge of homicide."

Kutnink flicked some cigaret ashes on the floor and swung back in his swivel chair. "That's right, Lieutenant. So what have you turned up?"

If I had ever had any, I lost all my sympathy for Kutnink. He was sitting there at his big desk with a federal officer behind him, some guy who, no matter how competent he might be, was an outsider, and in front of both the outsider and me, a murder suspect in the case at hand, he was needling Donovan. He was asking for it.

Donovan's tone didn't change. "I ain't turned up

nothin'," he said, "because for the last three hours, I been personally escorting this prisoner around here and there because you ain't got around to makin' any legal disposition of him."

Kutnink was a very tired man. "You think it's time to instruct me in the law, Lieutenant?" he said.

"No, sir, Mr. Kutnink."

He scored with that one. Kutnink shuddered lightly.

"I don't know who you got on your back in this," Donovan said stolidly, "and I guess it ain't my business. But I know the book and you must know it too. We got a regular procedure to handle things. Mostly it works. It's a wonder to me this bird dog ain't home in bed right now. Any law student could of got him there without hardly raising his voice."

"I seem to remember," Kutnink said, "that you and this bird dog are old friends. That wouldn't have anything to do with your attitude, would it?"

I thought someone might warn Kutnink to keep in condition.

"It happens I know him," Donovan said. "I know some things about him. I got nothing against him, but if he killed this—Kadek, I got nothing for him either. If you got a case against him and I can make it better, I'll do it. But you better let me lock him up and get goin' instead of standin' around playin' politics with him."

Kutnink pushed himself to his feet and ground out his cigaret in an ash tray. I found myself wondering about Donovan's hesitation over the name.

"All right, Lieutenant," Kutnink was saying. "Let's not be naïve. You're a policeman—I'm a politician.

We're supposed to work together. But it's not quite even. You don't have to worry about my part of the job, but I have to worry about yours. That's why I get paid more than you do."

He supported himself with one hand flat on the desk, dug out a new cigaret and got it lighted.

"A man has been shot to death. Immigration is mixed up in it. There's politics in it. In the vernacular, it's hot. It's hot for other reasons, too. I don't know all the angles, but this private eye knows some of them. It's up to you to get information out of him. I want to hear it as it comes, so we might as well get started."

Donovan's voice was, if possible, even flatter than before. "How you want me to get it?" he said. "You can't slap it out of him; I seen that tried. You can't threaten him with nothing more than a trial. You already tore up his license. What do you want me to do? hold him upside down and shake it out of him?"

Kutnink leaned on the desk, glaring at him, and Donovan looked back out of his black eyes. They were pretty evenly matched. Kutnink couldn't fire Donovan, or even break him, without facing a deadly retaliation. On the other hand, there wasn't much Donovan could do to Kutnink either. Only a politician could remove Kutnink.

Still, Donovan had a slight advantage. Kutnink had begun to look a little silly in front of company. Donovan hadn't been battling for me, but for the force and himself, in the ancient, endless feud. I was in the middle, but could at least try to look after myself. It seemed that maybe the time had come.

I backed away from Donovan and sat down with my

head in my hands. As I had expected, it got to Kutnink.

"Stand up!" he barked.

I raised my face and looked at him. "Up yours, Kutnink," I said.

He started around the desk and I stood up. He glanced at Donovan, who stood still.

"Why don't you tell the rest of it, Kutnink?" I said to him. "Why don't you tell them you don't want to book me because that would let a lawyer in between us? Why don't you mention Roscoe Turner and his powerful friends? Why don't you admit you can't hold me legally because I can get out on bail for any real charge you've got?" I started counting on my fingers. "Accessory after the fact, withholding evidence, obstructing justice, assaulting an officer——"

"You keep quiet!" he yelled.

"I don't have to keep quiet!" I yelled back at him. "I don't have to call you 'Mister,' the way Donovan does. I don't work for you, Kutnink. You work for me, remember?"

I pointed to the federal man in the chair. "And the same goes for you."

He blinked at me.

"You're on *my* payroll," I said. "The only way you can change that is to convict me of a felony. But you have to get that done first. I'm as free as when I came in here last night—freer, because then I had shackles.

"You can't convict me of a felony in this room. You've got to go through the regular routine. You had me down here since midnight last night, playing games with a prosecutor so incompetent he could qualify as a mental defective. I had enough. I'm leaving. You can pick me up and bring me back, but sooner or later you got to throw me in the can or let some judge set bail."

Kutnink tramped to his desk and picked up a telephone. "All right," he said, "if that's the way——"

"And one more thing," I said, "as soon as you start the routine, I'm going to have Larry Fisher up here, with reporters."

He put the phone down.

"I've got a good story, with substantiating evidence, about Roscoe Turner and his phony investigation of Lorraine Kadek. It's a hot one because it ties right in with this killing and they'll play it big. There are different ways to tell it. If I have to tell it through a mouthpiece—especially a real sharp one like Fisher—it might get garbled up some."

I headed for the door.

"Lieutenant!" Kutnink barked.

I heard Donovan's heavy tread, then a clearing of the throat. I looked back from the door and the federal man had shifted in his chair.

"Mr. Kutnink—" he said, "could we talk for a minute?"

Kutnink jerked around and leaned toward him to listen. Donovan stood near me at the door, examining his fingertips. The whispered conversation went on and on. I got Donovan's attention and spoke so it would carry across the room.

"Does it smell funny to you in here?" I said. He stared at me curiously. "You know how police states get born? Right in rooms like this, with this smell in them. The administrative smell——"

Kutnink wheeled. "Shut up!" He fumbled for a

cigaret and flopped into his chair. "Get out of here, the two of you," he said.

I was glad to go and I think Donovan was glad to follow me. We went through the waiting room and started down the quiet corridor.

"You don't talk very respectful to the officers," he said.

"I don't have to! I'm not bound to respect them—or any other official person—not by law or tradition or anything else!" I heard the echo of my shouting and lowered my voice as we went on to the elevator. "I don't mean to bore you," I said, "but people keep forgetting —it's the office you respect, not the guy in it. It's not the guy in the uniform—he might be a son of a bitch. It's not even the uniform. It's the idea behind the uniform——"

"All right," he said, "so you got no respect for people."

"I didn't say that!"

We rode down the shaft and walked some more halls. At the main desk, Donovan stopped and talked to somebody, while I hung around, waiting. Pretty soon he looked at me as if for the first time.

"What do you want?" he said.

"I'm not in custody?"

"I guess not."

A guy in the straight chair by the wall was folding a newspaper, stuffing it in his coat pocket. He would be my silent and, theoretically, unseen companion for as long as it should take to pry a lead out of me. But Donovan and I knew mutually that neither of us was fooled.

"Why don't you put Kutnink on my tail?" I said. "Learn him something."

"Good-by, dreamer," he said.

"Good-by, copper."

33.

From a cafeteria phone booth I called Georgiana. Somebody else answered and I asked whether there was a message for me. She said yes and read it to me:

"Esther Jarvis checked out of the Allen Hotel on the South Side about eight o'clock this morning. There was a small girl with her. She left no forwarding address. She was driving a three-year-old sedan. She paid for the room when she checked out. P.S. I forgot to get a description. P.P.S. No, I didn't forget."

"When do you expect Miss Hennessey?" I asked.

"I couldn't say."

"Thank you."

I hung up, bought a cup of coffee and nursed it, staring at the street window. I couldn't focus on it. It was all steam and shadows. There was no way I could start through those streets looking for Trudy Kadek. I wondered whether Georgiana had called Miss Colby, then decided she wouldn't have done that without checking with me first. She hadn't found much to report. Also, she would be sore at me, with some cause, and there was nothing I could do about that either.

Outside, I found a cab and directed it to my office. Crossing the bridge, I thought about the wreckage O'Connell and Robinson had made of it and asked the driver to take me to my car. He pulled in behind it and waited.

When I opened the door, some of the broken glass fell out. I pulled the seat forward and the box with the wires in it was gone. In its place was a sealed manila envelope, blank and clean. There didn't seem to be much inside it. I took it with me to the cab and directed the driver to a small hotel in my neighborhood. I checked in there, ordered a bottle sent up and took a long shower. Then I climbed into bed, opened the manila envelope and started through Turner's file on Lorraine Kadek. I didn't like the feeling of the neatly type-written sheets of paper. It was like handling garbage. . . .

The record went back to her college days. She was a good student, shy and retiring and not well known on the campus. In her last year she dated a boy named Bud Phelps. Her sister, Esther Jarvis, an office worker in Chicago, sent her money regularly.

Taught school in Fairmont two yrs., 1948 and '49. Record satisfactory. Visited Chicago summer '49; companion Phelps, later Kadek. Sex relations no confirm.

Sporting of Turner, I thought.

Not that he hadn't tried. There were plenty of other details of that summer, some of which I had heard, many of which not. The words had begun to blur on me and I skimmed through them, finding nothing.

Married Kadek Sept. '49, I read. *Phelps and Esther*

Jarvis attended. Honeymoon Lake Geneva, Wis. Following, Phelps frequent visitor to household, which included Esther J. Friction over sister-in-law confirm.

There was a string of miscellaneous items, none of which helped to bring Lorraine Kadek and her household truly to life and most of which would be of dubious accuracy, since the only way such information can be gathered is by interviewing neighbors and casual acquaintances and the passing of time wreaks havoc with the human memory.

Jul. and Aug. '50 Kadek worked at Wis. resort. Lorraine accompanied, leaving Esther in city. Noisy farewell party Kadek apartment—police called by neighbors 3 A.M. but Lorraine and Kadek gone. Half dozen musicians and dates, incl. Phelps. No arrests.

Almost had something there, Turner, old boy. But they slipped out on you.

I plodded on, fighting sleep. There were longer gaps now in the chronology, as if Turner's leg man had given up, or at least grown tired. Phelps disappeared from the picture. Esther quit her job and settled down to keep house for little sister. Kadek worked steadily and got into no mischief.

Spring vacation, April 1951, I read, *Lorraine K. attended teacher's institute, Springfield. Confirm. Same time, Esther J. left Kadek to shift for self. Signs of marriage breakup.*

This item was at the bottom of a page and there followed a gap of more than a year—a huge hole in the report, unaccountable to me at the time. It picked up with Lorraine's application for a position at Miss

Colby's school and there were a few more sparse entries telling the story much as I had got it from Miss Colby herself.

I could no longer hold off sleep. I managed to stay alive long enough to stick the report back in the envelope and to leave a call with the switchboard operator for four-thirty in the afternoon. Then I allowed myself quietly, luxuriously to pass out.

The call woke me, sweating and tangled in the bedclothes, with a picture of Trudy Kadek sharply frightening in my mind. I tried to call Georgiana, but she hadn't come in yet and there was no message for me. I gave Miss Colby's number to the operator and the bell rang twelve times and no answer. Finally I called my answering service.

"Miss Colby called several times," she said. "She finally left this number. There've been several others——"

"I don't care about the others. What was that number again?"

She repeated it. It was a downtown number that looked familiar. I put in the call and while I waited for it to go through, did a little browsing in the directory. The number belonged to Sherry Turner.

"Yes?" Miss Colby said, answering.

"Mac," I said. "You left this number."

"It's good to hear from you. Thank you for finding Trudy and getting her home safely."

The instrument jumped in my hand and I shifted it.

"It was nothing," I said. "How is Miss Turner?"

There was a considerable silence.

"I don't know," she said quietly then. "I'm afraid for her—for myself too——"

"I'll come over," I said.

"Thank you. I couldn't have asked it."

I dressed and went down to the barbershop for a shave. I bought a new shirt in the haberdashery off the lobby. Through the window I could see Donovan's man, stolid and vacant faced, waiting.

Upstairs, I put on the shirt, tried once more vainly to reach Georgiana and picked up the envelope containing Turner's file on Mrs. Kadek. In my coat pocket was the wrinkled slip of paper on which Georgiana had written Trudy's birth date for me. I looked at it for a minute, then put it in the envelope with the report.

Back in the lobby again, I walked up to the shadow and handed him the envelope.

"When you run into Donovan," I told him, "he'll be interested in this."

He blinked a couple of times and watched me out. I found a cab and rode to Sherry Turner's apartment. There was no black sedan out front and the security boys were nowhere in sight. I found her name on the wall in the foyer and walked to an elevator. When I looked back, the man with the newspaper in his pocket was studying the names on the wall.

The indirect lighting in the carpeted hall was subdued and chaste. On the clean ivory panel of her door
hung a minute brass knocker. When I lifted and
dropped it, I could barely hear it myself. But it must
have sounded inside, because I had no time even to lift
it again before the door opened.

Miss Colby wore her working clothes—a plain dark
suit with white blouse and a cameo brooch. The slight
disarrangement of her hair and some faint shadows under her eyes were the only signs that she had been under
stress. She stepped back without a word and I went in
past her.

It was a medium-sized, medium expensive apartment
in a quiet, well-run place. There would be a clause in her
lease covering propriety of behavior and it would have
some teeth in it. The living-room windows looked out on
the lake and fifteen stories down, you could watch the
traffic on the Drive. A swinging door led to a kitchen on
one side and a closed door in the opposite wall would
open on a bedroom hall.

On a coffee table stood a brandy bottle, glasses and
ice in a silver bucket. Miss Colby nodded toward it and
I helped myself and sat down on a love seat.

"Where is she?" I asked.

She nodded at the closed door. "She may be sleeping."

She opened a dropleaf desk near the hall door, picked up a thin sheaf of legal-sized paper and brought it to me. It was a carbon copy of Sherry's statement to the D.A. I glanced at it and put it down.

"You don't want to read it?" she said.

"I'm pretty familiar with it." I looked around the room some. "She didn't even go down there to sign it, did she?" I asked.

"No. The attorney prepared it and she signed it. She didn't even read it until this afternoon."

I couldn't think of anything to say.

"She was desolate, Mac. She was sick about it when she learned——"

"I believe it."

"She's so young."

"I know."

"She called me at my office. She kept saying she had done this terrible thing and I was the only person she could think of to call. She said you were in jail and it was her fault."

"They never got around to putting me in jail and none of it was her fault really."

She kept pushing at her hair, trying to get some stray strands back in place.

"What do you think she ought to do?" she said.

"How much did she tell you?"

"Quite a lot. I don't know how much there is."

"She tell you she'd slept in Kadek's bed, and mine?"

"Yes, but——"

"Nothing happened. I think that's true, if you care. I know it's true for me. If she told you that much, she may have told all of it."

She got up and walked around. "Did she kill him?" she asked.

"No," I said.

"Is it perjury, what she said in this statement?"

"No. She didn't appear anywhere, take any oath. If you sign a confession even and then deny it, it's not perjury."

"Then what can they do to her, if she should change it?"

I thought about it unwillingly.

"They can give her a bad time," I said. "They can yell at her, call her a liar, try to get her upset so she'll say something they want to hear. They can hold her as a material witness, in jail or out on bail. She wouldn't have any trouble raising bail. But any way you look at it, they can make life very dingy for her temporarily."

I poured another shot.

"Who did kill him?" she asked suddenly.

I took a long pull at the brandy and set the glass on the table. "Why do you want to know?"

She shook her head a little wildly. "I don't want to know, but I have to. In a way, I think I deserve to know. I can't force you to tell me——"

"What makes you think I know?"

She smiled gamely. "I seem to have the idea you know everything."

It struck me wrong in the wrong place. It was wrong all around.

"That's not even flattery," I said. "That's hysterical, if you'll pardon the expression."

She turned away abruptly. "I'm sorry," she said.

I waited. I couldn't do anything else. It was a time at

which I should have been able to think of something. There was nothing wrong with her. She was an intelligent, thoughtful, brave woman and she had done nothing against me. She had offered to help me at a time when I could have used some help. But I couldn't help her now. I didn't have the vocabulary. The truth was, I didn't even have the inclination. I had been pushed around and hadn't got over it yet and I was taking it out on her. I knew as I did it I was taking it out on her. But I couldn't help it. Because at the same time, she was taking some things out on me. There was a hole in her life, as in mine. It was a time when we should have gone out and got drunk together and maybe wound up in the same bed—and I have a hunch she would have been pretty good. But neither of us could have done it and I guess we knew that too.

When I looked at her again she was crying a little, not trying to hide it. "I'm not really sorry," she said. "I'm a different generation. I'm old fashioned. I believe in things!"

"Miss Colby——"

"Forgive me. You believe in things, too—but differently, just as Sherry does." She pushed futilely at the loose strands of her hair. "I believe that honesty is the best policy—that truth will out—that good is stronger than evil——"

"It may be. In the long run——"

"I believe that when a girl like Sherry Turner has made a big mistake, she should own up to it, regardless of the consequences, and that if she does, it will be good for her soul! I don't know why I believe it. Even while I say it, I know it's too simple."

Sherry's voice came low and shockingly across the room. We looked simultaneously at the now open bedroom door and she was standing there with a light topcoat over her shoulders, holding a small bag and a pair of matching white gloves in one hand. Her hair had been neatly arranged and her face carefully made up. Only around her pinkly swollen eyes was there any sign that she had been upset. She stood very straight. I had no idea how long she had been there.

"In my father's world," she said slowly, "there are two kinds of people: his kind—right-thinking people; and all the others."

Miss Colby started toward her, then stopped.

"He got in trouble over his taxes one year and I asked him about honesty being the best policy. He got very angry. He said that was different, that I didn't understand about money."

She came on into the room and stood very straight and beautiful. I wondered what it was costing her.

"I said nothing happened between Karl and me, and that's true. But it would have, if it had been up to me. It was Karl who wouldn't——" She faltered, then went on with it. "I didn't kill him either, but I might have. I was furious with him—when he sent me out because some people were coming up—a man and a woman.

"I was boiling inside. I thought of ways to kill him, hurt him. I wanted to just go home and never see him again. But I didn't. I did just what he told me to do. I went out and I went back, the way I used to do everything my father told me to do."

She blinked her eyes rapidly, started to brush at them with her gloves, then refrained.

"Anyway," she said, "I didn't do it. But I thought about it and I might have. What's the difference between doing a thing and thinking it?"

"There's a lot of difference," I said. "If all the people were dead who had been wished dead, we wouldn't have much population."

Miss Colby looked at me and winced.

"I learned one thing," Sherry said. "I learned not to be in love with him. He kept trying to tell me, but I wouldn't listen. But I learned. He was still in love with his wife."

There was a knock at the door and after a moment of hesitation, Miss Colby went over and opened it. I heard the rumble of Donovan's voice in the hall. Miss Colby came back and Donovan was following her. Sherry watched him fixedly. He nodded shortly to me and looked at her.

"Miss Turner?"

"Yes," she said.

"Lieutenant Donovan, police. I have to ask you——"

I watched her face break up, the way it had broken in Kadek's apartment when I had found her there. She met his eyes for about thirty seconds, then tossed her head desperately and backed through the door into the bedroom hall. I was on my feet when Donovan started after her.

"Stay here a minute," I said. "She can't get out that way. And take off your hat."

He blinked and took his hat off with some reluctance. He doesn't have much hair on his head.

By the time I got through the door and got it shut,

Sherry was sagging against the wall by the bedroom, broken-faced and frightened.

"I can't, Mac," she whispered. "I just can't go through with it. What will they make me say?"

I couldn't honestly give her much reassurance.

"If you go with Lieutenant Donovan, you'll be in the best hands. They may yell at you, insult you. But they can't make you say anything."

She looked at me closely in the half light. One of her hands lifted toward my face, then dropped.

"What did they do to you?" she asked.

"Nothing. They bored me."

"They did something. It shows in your face."

"Not much and they won't do anything like it to you. I'll call the lawyer and get him to work. He may get there ahead of you. You don't have to talk to anybody."

Her mouth trembled. "But what if——?"

"You're on top of it now, Sherry. There's not much longer to hold out—a few hours."

She looked at me curiously. "You know, don't you?" she said. "You know all about it."

"I think so. Most of it."

"You don't hate me for what I did to you?"

"How you talk. I'm trying to work up enough nerve to ask you for a date. We could have dinner——"

Little by little she pushed herself straight against the wall and smiled. "When you get the nerve," she said, "I'm in the book."

"This I know."

"You know I had to do it this way—I don't know why exactly."

"Maybe I know why too. Someday we can talk it over."

"Someday——"

Faintly beyond the closed door I heard the low rumble of Donovan's voice. Miss Colby said a few words, but I couldn't make them out. Sherry was standing straight now. I put my hand on her arm and she smiled and drew away, squaring her shoulders.

"I'm all right now," she said. "Will you send me a bill?"

"Yes."

"And say hello to Miss Hennessey for me."

"She'll be glad to hear it."

She started down the hall, then turned back. "Maybe some night I could get a date and the four of us could go out. Okay that way, Mac?"

"Okay, Sherry. Good luck."

She opened the door and walked into the living room. Donovan got up, holding his hat, and I walked in past her.

"She'll go with you to Kutnink's office," I said. "I'm sending Larry Fisher over there."

"Uh-huh," he said.

"Lieutenant Donovan?" Sherry said. "I'm sorry about your fishing trip."

He blinked at her, then at me. "Oh——" he said, "well, I can always go fishin'."

Miss Colby stood with tightly folded hands. "Do you want me to go with you, Sherry?" she said.

"No, thank you," Sherry said. "You were wonderful to come. I'll call you——" She sagged suddenly and I got ready to start over with her, but she recovered almost at once and when she walked to the door, she looked as good as any I have ever seen.

Donovan's hand swallowed the doorknob. "I'll be around," he said.

"Don't hurry," I said.

He went out and closed the door.

While I was at the telephone, Miss Colby poured a couple of slugs of brandy.

What if she gets loaded on me? I couldn't help thinking.

I got hold of Larry Fisher somewhere in the halls of justice and after I had given him the rundown on Sherry, he said,

"Kutnink is very burned."

"You don't say."

"I think you're in line for an investigation. Can you stand it?"

"Look, will you get on over there and get to work? I'll call if I need you."

"I may not be in."

"I'll keep trying."

"All right, hothead."

I hung up. Miss Colby and I examined each other across our brandy snifters.

"Who found Trudy Kadek?" I asked.

Her eyes widened. "But—Lorraine called me, told me the girl had been found—she was going in to pick her up——"

When I said nothing, she said, "You didn't know?"

"And Esther? Was she found too?"

"No. Just Trudy."

I set down my glass, went to the door and stood there, fooling with my hat.

"Would you like me to see you home?" I asked.

"I'll stay," she said. "She'll want a hot meal when she comes home—or at least someone to talk to."

I started to put my hat on and there was a light knock at the door. After a moment I opened it.

He stood out there with his blond hair and his big knuckles, staring at us. It was several seconds before I could develop the presence of mind to nod him into the room and get the door shut behind him.

"Miss Colby——?" I said, and stopped.

He nodded to her gravely and held out a big hand. "Karl Kadek," he said quietly.

35.

I couldn't think of anything to say for a while. He wouldn't take a drink, just stood in the middle of the room, gazing around at it curiously. Miss Colby looked numb.

"I was never up here before," he said.

"What happened?" I asked him. "You finally lost your mind?"

"I couldn't stay there any more," he said. "I knew the police were coming. I got out by the back."

"How do you mean, you knew they were coming?"

He shrugged ponderously. "You get so you can tell."

I guessed that would be true enough.

"What did you have in mind to do?" I asked him.

"I don't know. I had to see if she was all right—Sherry, I mean. I didn't hear from her."

I poured a little brandy. Miss Colby sank into a chair and covered her eyes with her hand.

"She's all right," I said. "The police took her downtown."

He closed his eyes. "She's a good kid," he said.

"Like a ten-dollar gold piece in a bucket of brass slugs," I said. "You said a true word, Kadek. She went down the line for you from the beginning and she's still going."

Suddenly I wasn't sore at him any more.

"There was no other way, was there?" I said.

"I guess not. I should have found one. But I couldn't even take her home, because of those two guys her father had watching her. There was nothing much with us, you know. She would come to listen to me play and we got acquainted. She's young—kind of impressionable. She thought it was romantic that I was from Europe and had gone through some of that stuff——" He was looking at me strangely. "You seem to know all about it," he said. "Did she tell you?"

"Not once. She held the line for you. I put different things together."

"She felt real bad about you, last Friday, that night at the hotel——" '

"It's all over now."

He looked at his hands as if they were strangers to him, then sat down heavily across from me. Miss Colby sat numbly, listening.

"Sherry found out her father was trying to get me, through Lorraine. I didn't know till she told me. Sherry was romantic. She said if I was in trouble with her father, it was her fault and she would stick by me. She figured if she just moved in with me, her father wouldn't dare go ahead till he could get us apart."

"You tried to talk her out of it?"

"Sure. It was crazy. But it didn't seem so crazy to me as it probably would to you—over here. Crazier things than that went on in Europe and you got used to it. A girl would do that for a guy if she cared for him. I guess I was scared too; I almost had my citizenship. It comes up tomorrow."

I nodded. "So you let her do it," I said.

"Not exactly," he said stubbornly. "I told her we wouldn't do it. But last Friday night, when I was working at the hotel, she called you and got those two thugs off her back long enough to go to her own place and get some things. When I showed up at home later, she was there waiting for me, with a suitcase."

"You realized, naturally, she was carrying a torch for you."

"I guess so. I spent most of my time the next three days trying to talk her out of it. It was kind of tough. I told her I was a funny guy; I had been in love once and had got married and I still felt the same way."

"If one of the Immigration people had happened around with her there and the place in the condition it was in, that might have ruined your chances for good."

"I know, but I couldn't tell her that."

"All right."

"I don't know if it was the right thing to do but it's

done now. It might have worked out all right, too, if it hadn't been for the—thing that came up."

"You mean the Bud Phelps thing."

He nodded. "Phelps was in my hair a long time. He couldn't seem to get over it that Lorraine married me. He used to hang around our place—even when Lorraine and I were out. He would tease Esther. I had to throw him out a couple of times. Later we patched things up, shared a place sometimes when he wasn't working."

After a while he went on. "Anyway, Sherry was staying there with me and we seemed to be getting away with it, until the other night. I was working at the Bantam Club and Phelps came in—" he glanced at Miss Colby —"with this other person and said he had to talk to me. He was pretty upset. I couldn't talk to him in the club there so I gave him my key and told him to go on up to the place and I'd get off early and go talk to him."

"Did Sherry know what was going on?"

"Not exactly. When we got to the place, I told her I'd have to see these people alone, on a private matter."

"And she went along with it?"

"Yeah. I don't know where she went, but she had a package with her when she came back."

"And you went on up to your place."

"Uh-huh. Phelps was dead, still bleeding, maybe not quite dead. I tried to call a doctor, but he was out. There was this special doctor of Phelps's that knew about his blood type——"

"I beg your pardon?"

"He had that rare blood type—I don't know—O type, I guess. He used to sell it to the hospital once in a while when he needed money. It's all right to have it, but it's rough if you have a baby—if the kid's blood is mixed wrong——"

"Go ahead. You couldn't get the doctor."

"No, and I saw he was dead then. I couldn't think what to do. I just sat and stared at him."

"How did Sherry take it when she came back?"

"Pretty hard, but she got control before I did. When I started to call the police, she stopped me. She said they would think I did it and even when they found out I didn't, on account of the investigation and all—— Then I thought of this old trick—leaving my papers and all and letting them think I was the dead one."

"A great scheme."

"Well, it's the kind of thing you don't count on for much except time. Maybe it would take them long enough to identify him that I could get the citizenship. Then I'd have a chance."

"All right. I certainly went along with it."

"I left the papers and wallet. All I kept with me were the basic papers I had to have for the ceremony. I told Sherry I'd take her home, but she wouldn't go. She said she would stay, to give me a start. She just wouldn't leave. We couldn't stand around arguing——"

"So you went to Phelps's room and stayed there."

"That's right. You scared me plenty when you came around asking about Lorraine. I thought it was you, from what Sherry had told me, and I didn't know what you knew, or what had happened to her, and I couldn't ask."

"It was getting you down even then, wasn't it? You were so fed up with it that you tried to get me to discover the body and get things started."

He looked at his feet. "It was riding me. I think if it hadn't been for Phelps's piano, I'd have gone nuts."

Miss Colby got up suddenly, excused herself and left the room. Kadek watched her go, then looked at me again, moving his head slowly, carefully.

"You knew I wasn't Phelps when you came up there, didn't you?"

"I had some information about you and Phelps. You were a blond. The dead one had red hair."

"As simple as that?"

"Sometimes it's simple, often not. You seem to have been kind of off and on with Phelps. I don't quite get that."

He shrugged. "I guess I felt guilty about taking his girl. Then, I had a little something on him. I would never have used it, but it would ride him, so to show him there was no trouble in sight, I'd let him move in with me when he was broke or not working. But that didn't work out much." He glanced at the door through which Miss Colby had gone. "Phelps was—well, he liked the girls. He would bring them up to the place."

He met my eyes steadily. "I didn't run around myself. Sherry Turner is the only girl I've gone out with since I broke up with Lorraine. I don't mean that's such a great thing, but that's the way I've been living."

"You say you had something on Phelps."

"I can't tell you about that," he said.

"Until after tomorrow?"

"It's got nothing to do with that. I can't tell you."

I let some time pass. Miss Colby came back to the room and stood around.

"What did you plan to do now?" I asked him. "Between now and ten o'clock in the morning?"

"I don't know. I thought maybe some hotel—or I could just walk around——"

"You'll get picked up for sure that way."

I looked at Miss Colby. "Did you ever tell Lorraine that her husband had been killed?"

"Yes. After you called last night."

"How did she take it?"

"She wouldn't believe it. She simply said, 'That can't be true.'"

Kadek was leaning forward, staring at his feet. "I called Lorraine," he said, "and told her I was hiding out, that if she saw anything in the paper, not to believe it. So she knew."

"That's why she didn't want to put the police on the search for Trudy," I said.

Kadek straightened slowly.

"Trudy?"

"She's all right," I said. "She's with Lorraine. Esther took her away the other day."

"Esther did?"

"But I understand Trudy's back home now. I don't know all the details."

He got on his feet and walked slowly to the door. I went after him.

"If you go out there now," I said, "they'll have you in five minutes."

"But somebody has to——"

He broke off, glancing past me at Miss Colby.

"I'll do it," I said.

There was about a minute of total silence, and then,

quietly, we heard Miss Colby's unhoped for but somehow predictable speech.

"You'd better come home with me, Mr. Kadek. I seem
to be the only person not involved with the police."

Kadek turned his head to look at her. "Thank you,"
he said, "but I've been ducking behind women's skirts
long enough——"

"You'd better do it," I said. "It's not as if there were
something you could fight man to man. What you're up
against, you can either go along with it or try to outwit
it. You can't fight it—not till after tomorrow."

"Maybe, but I can't just sit around——"

"I think so. If Sherry can go down there and let
them yell at her and still keep her mouth shut, then you
can sit it out until time for court in the morning. It may
not work even so—they may challenge you because of
this thing—but if I didn't think you could hold out, I
wouldn't lift a finger to help you."

Miss Colby was putting on her hat and topcoat.

"Let me be gone a while," I said. "The cops are shad-
owing me. Nobody will pay any attention to you after
I'm gone."

Kadek opened his mouth, but couldn't say anything.
He held out his hand finally and I shook it. Then I got
the door open.

"I'll trust you with each other," I said. "Play gin
rummy or something."

Miss Colby came to the door. "There's a lot I ought
to tell you," she said, "but I don't know how."

"One of these days," I said, "I'll give you a ring."

"I'll always be in."

"We'll try to keep the lines open."

"Don't you know it!"

I left her and went down in the elevator and out to the street. The man with the newspaper was standing on the opposite side, leaning against a tree. A taxi drifted around the corner and I flagged it. He started to fold his paper as I crossed toward him.

"Want to ride over with me?" I said. "You must be tired."

He looked startled, then sheepish, then grateful. "Well, yeah, Mac, if you don't mind. My feet are killing me."

We got in the taxi and I directed the driver to Tony's. The cop sat back, looking out the window. There wasn't much to look at. It was too early to be dark, but the fog had come in again and everything looked dismal and dirty. After a couple of blocks, he said, "Who was that doll Donovan came out with?"

"Some girl," I said.

"Brother! If I ever make lieutenant——"

"You wouldn't like it," I said. "Think of Donovan with that doll. All he gets is to turn her over to the lawyers. Then he gets to give her a ride home. What's in it?"

He thought it over. "I never thought of it that way," he said.

The driver pulled in opposite Tony's. We got out and I paid the fare.

"Come on in," I said, "I'll buy you a drink."

We started across the street and I glanced at the office window.

"On second thought," I said, "I'll have to join you later. Some dumb flatfoot—begging your pardon—left my light on."

I opened the door and yelled at Tony to set him up.

"If you sit in the front booth," I said, "you can keep an eye on my office door. Okay?"

"Yeah. Thanks, Mac."

I crossed toward the office, steeling myself to face the littered rooms. Well, I thought, I don't have to stay. I can go back to Tony's and spend the night there.

The door was unlocked. I opened it slowly and looked in.

There wasn't any litter on the floor. The top of the desk was clean. The light I had seen through the blinds was not from the ceiling light the cops had left on; it was my desk lamp. There was a fresh odor in the room, a faint fragrance of toilet water.

Georgiana was lying on the sofa, covered with a blanket, sound asleep.

36.

I tiptoed to the bedroom and it had been cleaned up too. The bed had been made with fresh sheets. A tall lamp on the bedside table burned dimly.

The kitchen was likewise immaculate. On a chair beyond the foot of the bed was a small overnight bag. I lifted the cover and looked in and there were some clothes, a woman's suit and some stockings and a smock. I wondered what she had on under the blanket.

I went back to the office, sat down at the desk and waited for her to wake up. She looked good sleeping. Her face was relaxed and the dim light softened and rounded its contours so that she seemed girlish and un-touched. A few strands of her blond hair had drifted across her forehead and in her sleep, she reached up and brushed at them. She moved slowly under the blanket, sighing.

On the desk lay a clean, slim file folder. I opened it silently and leaned close to read the message written in Georgiana's hand.

"One of your girl friends showed up in time for lunch. There wasn't much in the house, but luckily she settled for the breakfast of champions with canned apricots on top. She kept asking where you were and I kept saying you'd be coming pretty soon. It was a situation fraught with explosive potentials until she accepted the obvious fact that I was your mother.

"She came in a taxi that she had picked up some-where on the West Side and the driver parted from her without regret, mopping his nervous brow. He had done some fancy mental footwork, figuring out where she wanted to go. It was another lucky thing that I hap-pened to have the price of the fare which was $3.80—receipt herewith.

"After lunch she helped me clean the place up. I managed to convince her that if you had a mother, she must have one too, and I finally ran the woman to earth in some town out north and she said she would come and get Trudy—for this was her name—who then fell asleep.

"So came her mother—and here again was a very fraught situation—her mother being too pretty for my own good—until she appeared to take it for granted that I was your housekeeper.

"They seemed mutually disposed to wait for you but I explained that you were in jail for impersonating God and it might be twenty or thirty years before you could make it.

"So if you should come and find me sleeping, just call me Mrs. Rip Van Winkle."

I closed the file and pushed it aside. I don't know whether the whisper of sound it made sliding across the scarred wood was what did it, but gradually Georgiana came awake. She opened her eyes, closed and opened them again and stretched bare arms out over the end of the sofa. She turned slowly and lay with her face turned to me and after a while I knew she was looking at me.

"Hi, Mac," she said sleepily.

"Hello, pardner. I thought you were sore at me."

"I never could hold a grudge. How was it out in the world for the last twenty years?"

"I don't remember. Not like this."

She lay now with both hands under her face, watching me. "Did they give you a bad time?"

"Not too bad."

"Larry Fisher called and told me they'd taken you in. When I couldn't get you this morning on the phone, I came over and the door was open. I went home and got my work clothes and came back."

"You're some girl."

"I didn't have anything else to do."

"May I buy you a drink?"

"If you'll leave the room so I can get up."

"Nothing under there at all?"

"A little—so little."

"Intimate and beautiful?"

"Maybe. Maybe later——"

I got up and headed for the kitchen. Halfway across the room I detoured to the sofa, leaned over her. Her long arms came up slowly and lay lightly on my shoulders. Her mouth moved silently.

" 'Later' is a bad word for us," I said.

"Yes."

"How thirsty are you?"

"Hardly at all."

"I seem to have an armful of blanket."

Pretty soon she said, "You're strong enough to cope with that——"

I began to cope with it and she came over, warm and yielding through a long kiss. Then unexpectedly, she stiffened, held me off with her hands on my chest, looking into my face. "Got to go now," she said.

I sat very still, trying to hold onto it, knowing I couldn't. "You have an appointment or something?"

"I'm an old-fashioned girl——"

"What if I said I never want you to go the rest of my life?"

"It would be a sweet thing to say."

After a while she said, "It's not finished yet, is it? There's something more you have to do."

"If there is—how did you know?"

"I could feel it. I don't know exactly, but somewhere along in there I could feel it."

There was no use trying to hold onto it then. I released her and went to the window and stood there, waiting, while she dressed. When I looked around she was standing in the bedroom doorway with her overnight bag. I reached for my hat.

"I have my own car," she said. "Don't bother——"

"I'll follow you in my car. Drive slowly on Michigan and I'll pick you up on the Drive."

"There's a tail on you?"

"Uh-huh."

She backed away and sat down on the bed, huddled and alone like a girl in the rain.

"Fine," she said. "So when I walk out of here——"

"Nothing. Leave the bag. It was a business call. They know we do business together."

"I'll bet they do now."

"You can go out the back way and around the block. They have eyes only for me."

"You trying to get rid of me now?"

I gave her a long look. "Let's not fight, huh?"

She came up from the bed, walked to me and looked me in the eyes. I reached for her and she came against me, hard and taut, and we kissed for a long time.

"All right," she said to my mouth. "Never. But don't follow me home."

"As you wish."

"I wish——"

She pushed away and went to the kitchen. At the back door she lingered, doing something to her hair. She looked around, smiling brightly, and said, "Well, good night. It's been a busy day."

The last two words got lost in her throat and she reached for the doorknob blindly. I opened it for her and she straightened, looking out.

"Next!" she said loud and clear.

I started after her then, but she walked off quickly down the areaway toward Chicago Avenue and pretty soon I turned back inside and locked the door.

I slid her overnight bag under the bed, turned off the

lamps, let myself out the front door and walked down the street to my car. I waited a minute or two and Georgiana came quickly to her car in front of the office and drove away. I drove slowly to the corner and turned toward Michigan.

I hadn't seen the man with the newspaper, but there was a stranger leaning against the lamppost in front of Tony's and he looked sober. I waved at him but he didn't respond. Somewhere behind me, someone else would pick up the tail with a car. But if I knew Donovan—and I had known Donovan a long time—nobody would interfere with me until I would have turned up something worth chewing on.

The wind blew cold through the broken window and I drove slowly, reluctant as the sputtering, half-warm engine of my car.

37.

In the warm, frayed lobby of the Allen Hotel, two elderly residents were asleep in overstuffed wing chairs, the wreckage of the daily papers strewn around their feet. The desk clerk was like them in appearance and condition, but all he had to sleep on was a high stool behind the narrow desk. He got down slowly, lamely, as I stepped up and asked for Miss Esther Jarvis.

He put on a pair of thick-lensed glasses and started through a card file, repeating the name to himself softly as he searched. His voice was like the rustling of old, dry paper.

"Esther Jarvis . . . here she is, let's see—she checked out this morning."

"Did she leave an address?" I asked him.

He studied the card carefully, replaced it in the file and moved to a cashier's cage beside the desk. Pretty soon he came back with a sheaf of printed bill forms and started fingering his way through them. It took a long time but he found the one he wanted, pulled it out and examined it.

"No address."

I drummed on the desk with my fingers. He took off his glasses and waited.

"Is that her bill you have?" I asked.

He nodded.

"I wonder if I could take a look at it. It's urgent that we find her."

"Well, sir——"

I took out my wallet and flashed my driver's license at him before he could get his glasses on. By the time he had leaned closer to read it, I had it back in my pocket.

"Missing persons," I said quietly. "I thought if she made any telephone calls, they might give us a lead."

"Oh," he said, "if you're from the police, of course——"

He pushed the form across the desk. I looked at it and there were half a dozen telephone calls to two different numbers. One appeared only once and had not been completed. The other was listed five times. I memorized the two numbers, both of which carried city exchanges. The address she had given the hotel was Lorraine Kadek's.

I gave the bill to him.

"She had a little girl with her," I said.

He nodded slowly. "Yes . . . I remember—a peculiar thing—the day clerk was complaining to me this afternoon: 'That crazy woman in three-oh-four kept asking me for this number and I kept telling her it was disconnected. At five o'clock in the morning!' "

"Was there anything else about her you remember?"

He thought about it. "No, I don't think so. I checked her in, last night. Quiet sort of woman, with the little girl. Plain looking woman."

I pushed away from the desk. "You've been a big help," I said.

He nodded gravely. "Any time, officer."

In the car, I drove faster now back to the North Side, my coat collar turned up against the wind. I couldn't tell whether the tail was with me or not, but it didn't matter really. It might just turn out that I would be glad to have them show up.

No, I thought then, not for a while yet.

Near Bughouse Square, I checked on my memory in a streetside telephone directory. The one-time number, the one on which she had got the disconnect reference, belonged to Bud Phelps. The other was Kadek's.

I wondered what she had said, five different times, to the cop who had answered the phone—and vice versa. Surely they had followed it up, but possibly she had been gone from the hotel by the time they had found it.

I drove past Phelps's building and there were no cops

in sight. I parked and walked to it and climbed the old stairs. There was no piano music. I knocked and waited and knocked again and nobody came. When I tried the knob, I found the door locked. I knocked some more and a door opened down the hall. A man in shirtsleeves looked out at me.

"Ain't home," he said.

"Thank you," I said. . . .

The time now was eleven o'clock. The street that Kadek's apartment faced was dark and empty. I made a slow U-turn at the corner and drifted back toward Kadek's building. The lights were on in that downstairs apartment and I decided those people must have a hell of a light bill. While I sat there thinking about it, the lights went out. But light still showed from the third floor.

I sat there for a long time, looking for cops—not behind me, not for the shadows—just for those few who might be hanging around the scene on orders. But they had had twenty-four hours now to go through it, remove the body and take from the place whatever might be useful later.

That Trudy, I thought, as I climbed out of the car. She must have got either scared or fed up and wandered away. There would have been a taxi and she had got into it.

Walking toward the building, my heels clicked loudly and I changed my stride to quiet them.

And it just so happened, I thought, that she ran into Georgiana. I wonder where she would have gone if Georgiana hadn't been there?

Well, I thought, the cabby would have thought of something.

He would have thought of the police.

And so it would have worked out in another way.

As before, nobody lurked in the shadows of the area-way. Nobody stood just inside the door, nor on the stairs, nor in the hall at the top, and there was a thread of yellow light, as before, but dimmer, and now, in addition to the light, there was the sound of music—quietly, as from a radio.

38.

I tried the door silently and it wasn't locked. I tapped on it, then twisted the knob and opened it an inch. The radio music sounded up, but nobody spoke to me. I looked in and the living room was deserted. I stepped inside and closed the door, slamming it lightly. There was a sound from the kitchen, metallic and dull. I counted to three.

"Karl!" she called. "Is that you?"

I stood there by the door, saying nothing. What would I have said?

She came out of the kitchen and through the dim hall, her high heels clicking on the floor. In the living-room light she stopped suddenly, looking at me with that squint.

"Hello——?" she said.

I managed to smile. "The door was open," I said, "I came on in——"

She took some more steps and stopped again, watching me. She wore a white, frilly apron over a black satin dress. The dress was skin tight and flagrantly revealing. I wondered whether she had made it, then decided not. She had a near-perfect figure. She wouldn't be hard to fit.

I kept smiling and she returned it fleetingly as she fought inside herself to make me fit.

"You're a friend of Karl's. I've been expecting you. Dinner is almost ready. Won't you sit down?"

I moved to the chair where Sherry had sat with her dress riding her thighs and she watched me steadily, her fingers smoothing and plucking, over and over, again and again, the crisp white apron.

"I can't imagine what's keeping Karl," she said. "He ought to be here any minute."

"Well, he's working at the club, isn't he? I didn't really expect him—just came on up. I hope it isn't inconvenient."

"Not at all. Everything is ready."

I couldn't keep looking at her. I let my eyes wander, looking at the blue-walled room, spotless, immaculate. Even the floor had been scrubbed. The venetian blinds gleamed ivory white in the lamplight.

When I looked at her again, she was gazing at something beyond me. Her lips moved, but there was no sound.

"I guess we haven't met," I said. "I've known Karl a long time. You're Esther, aren't you?"

Her face twisted, clouding, and I felt my tongue between my teeth.

"I'm Lorraine," she said. "Esther doesn't live with us any more."

"Oh. I was pretty mixed up. How's Trudy?"

She answered dully, suspicious now. "She fell asleep, waiting."

I sat there.

"Would you like a drink?" she said finally. "I think there's some wine."

"That would be fine. Let me help you."

She turned toward the kitchen and I followed. I glanced into the bathroom as I passed and saw how the chromium plated fixtures had been polished and gleamed brightly.

In the kitchen I remembered with shock the piles of dirty dishes, the overflowing wastebaskets, discarded bottles and lipstick-stained glasses; the army of ants parading across the dirty shelves. All this had been cleared away. The linoleum shone like a mirror. Even the stove had been cleaned, but there was nothing cooking on it, no odor of food. The refrigerator door was broad and white and gleaming and I knew as I knew my own name that inside it would be clean like everything around me—and empty.

Esther was taking a wine bottle from a cupboard. In it was maybe a finger and a half of cheap sherry. She looked at it with satisfaction and brought out three shining cocktail glasses.

"Allow me," I said.

She handed me the bottle.

"Thank you," she said. "I thought I heard Trudy

crying. I'd better look in." At the kitchen door she turned to me with a worried frown. "Be sure to save some for Karl."

"By all means."

I poured a thimble of the wine into each glass, picked up two of them and started back to the living room. The bedroom door was open and I saw her leaning over the made-up bed, fussing with a bundle of baby blankets. She was talking in a low, soothing voice, but I couldn't make out the words. I went on to the living room.

After a while she joined me. I handed her one of the glasses and she sat down with it, holding it loosely, twisting it slowly, continually with the fingers of both hands. Her lips were moving again and this time they made sound—a quiet, irregularly flowing stream of indistinguishable words. There were fluctuations of tempo and intensity, but not of tone. I had no way of knowing when it would be safe to interrupt.

"I heard about the fine thing you and Karl did," I said, taking a chance, "about Esther and Trudy."

The flow of words stopped and her eyes returned to me, watching.

"I mean," I said, "letting Esther use your name when she had the baby. I think it was a very unselfish thing to do."

So unselfish, I thought suddenly, that when Turner came across it, he left it out. How could it help his big case?

Esther shifted uneasily in her chair. "It was the least we could do," she said. "Esther had been so good to me. The baby had to have a name."

I looked into my empty wine glass. "Didn't the real father offer to help at all?"

"You see——" she said slowly, as if sighing—"we never knew who he really was——"

Her eyes left me as her voice sank to that running monotone, but louder now.

"He laughed . . . those nasty things . . . and laughing all the time telling dirty jokes . . . trying to put his hands on her . . . they try to make you do things . . . the things they said about me they told everybody in the office . . ."

I lost the words then and pretty soon she paused, trying to look at me. "I wonder what's keeping Karl?" she said. "He may be angry. There wasn't anything in the house. We'll have to eat out——"

I stood up, holding the wine glass. "I've got an idea," I said, trying to make it sound hearty. "Why don't I call Karl at the club and tell him to meet us at my place? It's close by. We can have a cocktail and then go out somewhere, to some nice place."

Her face brightened. I had never seen it like that. I went on, trying to hold her, make her stay with me. "I'll call him and we can go to that good place on Rush Street, the Bavarian place."

"That would be nice," she said.

I headed for the telephone and she came along.

"I'll get Trudy," she said.

I put on a laugh. It ached from my feet to my head. "I'd almost forgotten about Trudy," I said.

I picked up the phone and she went past me down the hall. I found the number of the neighborhood G.P. in my wallet and dialed it. By the time the connection was made, she was back from the bedroom with the bundle of baby blankets in her arms. She stood near me, waiting. The ringing started at the other end and she shifted the bundle slightly. Half hidden among the blankets was the wide-eyed, dead, staring face of a large doll, such as she might have bought in any drugstore. She wasn't talking now. She was listening, and watching.

It rang and rang and nobody answered. I held it with a moist hand, waiting.

You have to answer, I thought, soon now, right away. Come on, Doc. I can't keep her with me forever and if I lose her again——

She moved restlessly beside me and I shifted the thing to my other hand and smiled stiffly.

"You know how it is at the club," I said, "takes them forever to answer the phone if they're busy——"

She said nothing. I glanced at the big doll face under the blankets.

He can't be out on a call, I thought. The exchange service would answer for him.

She stared at me with a fixed look and I wondered who I was for her.

He came on then, freshly wakened, his voice hoarse and distant. I had to clear my throat in order to talk clearly to him while she stood listening.

"Hi there," I said, "Lorraine and I thought you'd like to meet us at my place—across from Tony's, you know? As soon as you can make it. What's that? . . . Oh, the tape on my chest—that second batch is still good."

She moved again and her eyes wandered. The doc was making some wise crack about jokes in the middle of the night and I cut into it, saying, "Fine then, you'll meet us there." I brought up a chuckle. "There'll be a light in the window."

I didn't want him there waiting for us. I wanted him later, but not much—as if it would be Karl coming.

When I hung up, she started across the living room with the bundle. I caught up with her and opened the door. She had no coat, but I couldn't take the chance of frustrating her. It would be a short ride.

In the hall I offered to carry Trudy, but she clutched the doll close and walked rapidly ahead of me down the stairs. When I opened the front door, she hesitated a moment, then went ahead.

At the sidewalk, she turned suddenly and started off away from my car. When I caught up with her, she was mumbling again. I put my hand on her arm and she stopped.

"Lorraine," I said, "the car is back here."

She turned her head slowly, looking both ways along the street.

"Yours is locked up and everything, isn't it?" I said.

"Yes."

"Mine's right over here. Let's take that."

She came along then, but pulled away from my hand and kept space between us back to the car. When I opened the door, she gave me a long, suspicious look, then climbed in reluctantly, arranging the doll blankets.

She sat jammed against the door and I drove slowly to cut down the blast of air through the broken window. But she didn't seem to notice the cold. Off and on she talked quietly to herself, but the intervals of silence grew longer and by the time I pulled up in front of the office, she had said nothing for some time. When I got around to the door and opened it, she came out without a word, exposing her knees carelessly as she swung her legs off the seat.

She held the doll carelessly now and went with me up the steps. Once she nearly dropped it and I helped her catch it and rearrange the blankets.

As I opened the outer door, making sure the night-latch was open, my eyes searched the street for the doc, but he was nowhere in sight. He would be waiting for the light in the window. He wasn't stupid. Sleepy, maybe, but not stupid.

I urged her through the vestibule and into the dark office. The doll bundle drooped in her arms.

"You want to put Trudy on the sofa?" I said.

I walked over there with her and she dropped the doll listlessly and turned away at once. I moved toward the desk lamp, reaching for it, but somehow she got in my way.

"Let's not turn on a light," she said.

"Well, it's pretty dark——"

"Please, no light. Just for a while."

"All right."

She couldn't have figured out my conversation with the doc, I thought. Then I thought, she's back now, for a while, all the way. She wouldn't want light. In a very special way, darkness had always been good to her.

I found her a chair and sat down at my desk. She sat down, too, crossing her legs, adjusting the tight skirt carelessly. She sat with her head back against the top of the chair. The dim light from the street fell favorably for her, lighting her from the neck down and leaving her head and face in shadow.

"I know you," she said after a minute. "You're that detective—Mac."

39.

We fell into a well of silence, out of which I climbed slowly to reach for the telephone.

"Whom are you calling?" she said.

"I thought I'd check in with my answering service."

I dialed and waited. The girl came on and when I identified myself, she started in with the apology routine again.

"Forget it," I said. "Nobody got hurt much. Any calls?"

"Not since the last time you checked. Listen, if the police should come again——"

"I don't think they will, but if they should, now or in the future, tell them nothing. Refer them to me. You can be subpoenaed as a witness and that's all. Nobody is bound, legally or morally, to divulge confidential information informally—nobody, to anybody, any time, any place."

"I know——"

"It's well to remember that. Gives you a little peace of mind."

"Thank you."

"I'll be in for a while."

"All right."

I hung up. Esther Jarvis hadn't changed her position. I tried to think of a way to talk to her.

"You're awfully sure of yourself, aren't you?" she said.

"Not especially."

"I admire sureness."

"I don't know that it's sureness, if you were referring to my conversation. In a free country you have to live like a free man. If you live another way, you're a traitor to the country as well as to yourself. People have certain rights—privileges too, but also rights. Legal rights and moral rights don't always jibe. Sometimes you have to make your own decisions."

"Even if it means going outside the law?"

"The law isn't perfect. If you break it, you have to expect to pay for it one way or another. Sometimes a man will take that chance, for his own reasons."

This can't go on for long, I thought. Something—maybe the cold ride over here, the new environment, something I had done or said—had brought her back. But it couldn't be for long. You couldn't do it that way.

"What you're saying is," she said, "the end justifies the means."

"Not at all. You have a personal responsibility not to betray yourself or society. If every law were perfect and covered every possible contingency and if the goal of every law were a constructive goal, then there wouldn't be any problem. We wouldn't even need a Supreme Court. There wouldn't be any tests.

"It's not a question of 'goodness' or 'badness.' There

weren't many 'good' reasons for breaking the prohibition law. It was a stupid law, stupidly drawn, but the reasons for breaking it weren't so good either, except when they were revolutionary. They were destructive reasons."

I stopped talking. Suddenly it seemed to me that I had been talking forever in a dark circle—to Catherine Colby, to Lorraine Kadek, to Donovan, Turner, Kutnink, to Sherry Turner—and a circle has no end.

"Could I have a drink?" she asked suddenly.

"Of course."

I found my way through the dark room to the kitchen and back, with a bottle, ice and glasses. She had changed her position slightly, but still sat with her head back and her hands in her lap. They were far from relaxed. She kept twisting them together, rubbing them, one with the other.

I poured a couple of small shots over ice. She went through hers in a hurry and I gave her some more. Gradually her hands relaxed.

"Why did they take Trudy away from me?" she said.

I began to feel afraid of the dark. It was an old, half-forgotten feeling. She held out her glass and I poured a little more whisky in it.

"That was a silly thing to say, wasn't it?" she said.

"I don't think so."

I moved and my chair creaked.

"Could we just sit here a while?" she said quickly. "I'm so tired."

"Would you like to lie down in the other room?"

"Maybe, pretty soon. It's so peaceful here."

After a while she said, "It's more than just peaceful. There's a feeling of strength. I admire strength— strong people. Tonight I feel strong."

"It could be the whisky," I said.

"That was unkind."

"I'm sorry."

She finished the drink and turned the glass slowly between her hands.

"Maybe that's part of your strength," she said. "Maybe you have to be unkind sometimes to—maintain your position."

"I don't think so."

The glass in her hands froze into stillness. She raised it slowly over her head, then threw it hard on the floor. It broke, crashing. My fingers were painfully stiff on the arms of my chair.

"Do we have to argue all the time?" she said harshly. "Do you have to deny everything I say?"

I kept quiet. After what seemed like a very long time, she got out of the chair, pouring out of it as if all her bones had broken, and crawled on her hands and knees to where the glass had splintered. Slowly she began picking up the pieces, groping for them in the dark. I went to her and touched her shoulder.

"Let it go," I said. "No harm done."

She stiffened under my touch and remained half crouched, holding the pieces of glass in one hand. Her fingers were bleeding slightly. When I reached down, she let me take the glass. I tossed it in the wastebasket, took her arm and got her on her feet.

"How about that rest?"

"All right."

I switched on the desk lamp quickly and she made no protest. She let me lead her toward the bedroom door, then stopped, staring at the sofa.

"They took Trudy away," she said. "Why? Trudy was mine."

"Trudy is perfectly all right," I said.

"How would you know?"

"Would you like to call Lorraine on the phone——?"

She spoke now with strident hostility.

"You know everything, don't you? You're a detective —a regular Sherlock Holmes! I'll bet you even looked up Trudy's birth certificate."

"That's only a piece of paper, Miss Jarvis——"

Her hands twisted sharply at her dress and she backed quickly into the bedroom. A light went up brightly. I heard footsteps out front and turned to head for the door, but then she was yelling at me from the bedroom.

"Sherlock! Come in here!"

As I passed the sofa on the way in there, I heard the office door open behind me. I didn't take time to look around. She yelled at me again when I pushed through the bedroom door.

"I'll show you whose baby she is!"

She was standing with her feet planted firmly, a little apart. All she had on was her shoes and stockings. All she bothered to cover was her face with both hands. In the sudden light, she looked like a living model for a modern Venus in marble; her body was that beautiful. Also, unmistakably, it was the body of a mother.

She spoke through her hands. "Take a good look. Does it look like a name on a legal document?"

"Of course not," I said quietly.

Behind me in the office I heard the faint snap as the doctor opened his bag.

She began to cry, sobbing into her hands, and her big body slumped wearily. I took her arm and led her toward the bed. She came along all right to the edge of it, then stiffened and pulled away. Her eyes fell on the lamp beside the bed and her face twisted violently. She swept out with one hand and knocked the lamp to the floor. It broke and the light went out.

When I moved my hand to urge her down on the bed, she started to fight. The doctor was in the room now and I saw him slip something into his pocket as he moved in to help me. She was very strong and it took the two of us to get her on the bed and stretched out and covered. Even then she went on fighting and I sat near her head, holding both her arms, massaging them gently. Little by little she quieted. The doctor backed off with his hand in his pocket. Her arms writhed in my hands and I held them and said, "It's all right, Lorraine. Beautiful Lorraine."

She stopped twisting, but she was trembling now and I pulled the blanket up around her. She moved under it, trying to draw her knees up and when I let go of her arms, she turned heavily and lay with her head in my lap. I began to massage her shoulders and back, feeling the knots of tension soften under my hands. She had taken up the mumbling again, but all I could make out was brief snatches of words without context.

The doctor stood near the bed and I saw that he had a needle in his hand. I shook my head, growling, "Something orally, Doc."

He shrugged and turned away and a moment later I heard him in the kitchen.

". . . said I was beautiful . . ." she was saying. "Lorraine's beautiful—not Esther . . . they made me do bad things . . . things and they laughed . . . little boys do bad things . . ."

The doctor came back, holding a glass of water and a couple of red capsules. I lifted her head and slid my arm under her shoulders. She looked at me and her eyes were straight and I wondered again who I was for her.

"Beautiful Lorraine," I said. "We won't let any boys do bad things. But you have to get over that cold."

The doctor put the capsules in my hand and she looked at them carefully. After a minute, she opened her mouth and let me put them in. The doctor gave me the water and I held the glass for her while she drank. When she had finished with it, he took the glass away, left the room and closed the door.

I let her down again and she started the talking. It came very softly now and slowly and I kept up the massage until she lay quietly in the bed and her mouth was still. When I moved to leave her, she stirred some under the blanket, but remained asleep. I waited by the door for a while, watching her, then got it open and went out to the office.

40

The doctor was standing beside the desk with a glass in his hand. I sat down in my desk chair.

"I helped myself to a drink," he said.

"Sure."

"You could probably use a stiff one yourself."

"No."

"My off-hand diagnosis would be that the woman has flipped."

I didn't say anything. He finished his drink and reached into his pocket. I became aware that he was looking at me expectantly and managed to remember who he was.

"She killed a guy," I said. "He did her wrong and she killed him. He shouldn't have laughed at her."

He cleared his throat faintly and rustled the paper of a note pad. "It shouldn't be hard to prove insanity," he said.

"No, that won't be hard."

He cleared his throat again. "I'd better call the hospital first, then the police——"

"Not yet."

He raised his head quickly, staring at me.

"I have to, Mac. You know that."

"She's asleep, isn't she? She's making no trouble."

"That's not the point."

"Not yet," I said. "I'll take the responsibility."

There was a pause.

"Sure you wouldn't like a drink?" he said.

"Because part of the reason she killed him is a guy who is sitting around with his fingers in his mouth, waiting to get to be a citizen of the United States. That can't happen till ten o'clock tomorrow morning and I don't want any official people putting their mouths to her before that. That much I can do for her—and him."

I heard him sigh, move to the sofa and sit down heavily.

"Thanks for coming," I said. "I'll pay for it. If you want to go back to bed——"

"It's up to you," he said, "but you might have some trouble. That stuff I gave her won't last forever. If I had used the syringe——"

"I couldn't let you do it!"

He kept quiet. I didn't want him quiet. I wanted him to say something so I could fight with him. I slammed my hand down on the desk so it hurt to my elbow.

"Our society is the most stupid, the most brutal in the world," I told him. "You ask for love and you get a needle. You ask for relief from a private horror and you get clamps on the head or a drill in the skull. You ask for understanding and somebody sells you a book on the power of positive thinking!"

I stopped. I had begun to shout.

"You better have a couple of those pills yourself," he said quietly.

"No. I'll be all right now. Go ahead, get some sleep. Don't worry about the bundle. It's only a doll."

I sat in the chair, holding myself tight inside. I would have to stop talking like that. People didn't like you to talk that way.

. . . little boys do bad things . . .

I poured myself a shot and drank it. The doctor stretched out on the sofa and went to sleep. I admired the way he could do it, but guessed it was something you would learn all right.

When the knock sounded on the office door, I knew, the way you sometimes know when the telephone rings, who it would be. It would be about that time now. The doctor moved on the sofa, but went on sleeping and I walked quietly to the door and opened it. Donovan was there alone in the vestibule, holding a beat-up manila envelope. I went out with him, closing the door behind me.

"I've got company—sleeping," I said.

He was in no friendly mood. He waved the envelope in my face. "It's time to talk," he said. "You start."

I pushed past him and sat down on the steps while he leaned against the street door, wide and heavy, waiting.

"How did you make out with Miss Turner?" I said.

"Don't ask nothing. Just tell me."

He wasn't fooling. They were riding him hard now, with spurs—Kutnink, the D.A., the Commission, the federal people. He was tough, but any horse can be broken.

"The dead one was named Bud Phelps——"

"We knew that when I had you in Kutnink's office," he said. "Get on with it."

"He was a great lover type. He got Esther Jarvis pregnant. She was a pushover. If you would spend a few minutes with her, you'd know it—or once you would have known it. The little girl had to be Esther's, not

Lorraine's. She was born in Danville, at a time when Lorraine was at some teachers' meeting in Springfield. It wouldn't be any problem for Esther to enter the hospital under Lorraine's name. You don't have to take an oath to get a baby delivered. Not yet you don't."

There was a little silence and Donovan said, "All right. How did you know Phelps fathered the kid?"

"It couldn't have been Kadek, because he was working out of town at the time it would have to happen. It didn't have to be Phelps, but it must have been. He had a rare blood type, used to pick up a few dollars once in a while selling it to hospitals. The little girl was born with an RH factor that Phelps's type, with Esther's, would produce. You'll never be able to prove it, but so what? Phelps is dead and Esther Jarvis is no longer able to set you straight on anything."

He kept quiet this time, just waited.

"Esther had pretty well loused up her sister's marriage. When Turner started in on Lorraine, Esther saw that the teaching job could be lost and so would their home. Esther was no longer independent, and she couldn't leave the little girl. There was only one person to turn to—Phelps. And when she caught up with him, the only one for Phelps to turn to was Kadek, who had taken care of him for years in one way and another— even assuming the role as Trudy's father, for Lorraine's sake. It was the dirtiest thing Phelps could have done to him, to drag him into it at that time. But Kadek came through, as always, tried to help, sent Esther and Phelps up to his own place."

Donovan shifted his weight impatiently.

"They must have got in the fight as soon as they got

there. She had Kadek's gun that Lorraine had taken
when they separated. She must have figured on using it
to scare him. I don't know whether she did or not.
Maybe it went off before she knew what she was doing.
Maybe he laughed at her. In her condition, that could
have triggered her. I did it to her myself, only then she
didn't have a gun."

"Why didn't Kadek call the cops?"

I looked at him, blinking to find him against the glass
door with the gray street light behind his bulk.

"Would you," I said, "under the circumstances?"

"Where's Kadek now?"

"You'll have to find him. I'll keep him running till
ten in the morning if I have to."

"Where's the Jarvis woman?"

"She's asleep in my bed."

He pushed away from the door with his feet planted.
"We'll go in and talk to her."

I got up slowly from the step, feeling the muscles
tighten in my stomach, hating it.

"No," I said. "We'll give her a break—and Kadek.
One of the few breaks either one of them ever got."

"Kadek will never make it in the morning. They got
a federal guy waiting to meet him at the door."

"You can call him off."

"No, I can't and you know it."

"You can try, and I'll help. It's the only help you'll
get from me. You can get Kutnink on the phone—or
one of the Commissioners. You can tell them you've got
Phelps's murderer, that Kadek had nothing to do with
it. You can explain to them that if Kadek doesn't make
citizenship in the morning, the most they can do will be

to deport him. If they have to haul him up on an accessory charge or a failure to notify—they'd better make a citizen out of him first. Give them more jurisdiction. They love that jurisdiction."

He took a step toward me and I braced against it automatically, facing him.

"You goin' to try to read me speeches till ten o'clock?" he said. "I'm a cop on duty. I'm goin' in there."

"Then you'll have to get a warrant. And if you get back with it before ten o'clock, warrant or no, I'll fight you. I'd hate it, but I'll do it and maybe you can still lick me. But it will take some time and maybe long enough."

He shifted his feet and his right arm moved. It could come any moment now; he could let go at me. It would hurt. And when I would hit back at him, that would hurt even more. He had brought me up, trained me, fought for me, on the force and off. The only times I had ever hit him were in a formal way, for fun, in the gym.

"I'm not quite alone," I told him. "I'm on a team." Maybe it was the tension that made me laugh a little, so that he shifted his weight again and thrust his big head forward, staring at me. "If you get past me, you'll have to fight every one of the others—Sherry, Catherine, Lorraine and Georgiana—and every one of them is as tough as you or me."

I don't know how long he stood there, leaning toward me, staring through the dim light. I know the fingers of my right hand were stiff from the strain of holding them clenched and ready. I know that something clicked in my mind as we reached the point at which he had waited too long, the point at which he had decided not to slug it out. He settled back almost imperceptibly, took off his hat and punched it some and put it on again, then turned slowly to look out through the glass of the door.

"You want to use my phone?" I asked.

He looked at me for a moment, then shook his head, opened the door and went out. I waited quite a long time, until long after the sound of his tread had faded, then turned back into the office. The doctor was sleeping soundly, quietly.

I must have slept myself, in the chair, waking now and then with a jerk in time to catch myself tipping too far back. Morning light had begun to fill the room when I got up stiffly, went to the bedroom and looked in at her. She was moving restlessly in the bed and I woke the doctor and got two more pills from him.

She protested weakly, but when I held her against me and spoke quietly, massaging her back easily and gently, she took them all right. I stayed with her until she was quiet again. When I got up from the bed, she didn't stir. I glanced through the open door into the office, leaned over quickly and kissed her face, then moved away hastily for fear the doctor might have seen me. But when I returned to the office he was still asleep.

I slept again in the chair and when I woke it was light, there was the sound of mid-morning traffic in the street and the doctor was sitting up, rubbing his face with both hands. We said nothing to each other. There wasn't a hell of a lot to be said.

I looked out the front window and they were changing the guard. A car had pulled up near Tony's front door and two of its doors were open. A couple of cops stood on the walk. One of them shrugged and climbed into the car. The other walked slowly up the street past Tony's, stretched his arms and started back. One of the car doors closed. A third man got out of the car. It was Donovan. He walked down and talked for a while to the new shadow and the car pulled away and disappeared. Donovan looked at his watch and I looked at my own. It was five minutes to ten.

I went outside and stood on the steps for a while. Donovan looked at his watch again. After a minute or two he left the shadow and started across the street toward me. By my own watch, it was one minute after ten.

He looked big, coming, and unbreakable and I knew this was true about him. He was unbreakable. He had been broken and he had mended and the new joint was stronger than before. There was the crude blast of a truck horn on Michigan Avenue and he kept coming. . . .

FINE MYSTERY AND SUSPENSE
TITLES FROM CARROLL & GRAF

☐ Allen, Henry/FOOL'S MERCY $3.95
☐ Blanc, Suzanne/THE GREEN STONE $3.50
☐ Brand, Christianna/FOG OF DOUBT $3.50
☐ Browne, Howard/THIN AIR $3.50
☐ Boucher, Anthony/THE CASE OF THE BAKER
    STREET IRREGULARS $3.95
☐ Boucher, Anthony (ed.)/FOUR AND TWENTY
    BLOODHOUNDS $3.95
☐ Buell, John/THE SHREWSDALE EXIT $3.50
☐ Carr, John Dickson/THE EMPEROR'S
    SNUFF-BOX $3.50
☐ Carr, John Dickson/LOST GALLOWS $3.50
☐ Coles, Manning/NIGHT TRAIN TO PARIS $3.50
☐ Coles, Manning/NO ENTRY $3.50
☐ Dewey, Thomas B./THE BRAVE, BAD GIRLS $3.50
☐ Dewey, Thomas B./DEADLINE $3.50
☐ Dewey, Thomas B./THE MEAN STREETS $3.50
☐ Dewey, Thomas B./A SAD SONG SINGING $3.50
☐ Dickson, Carter/THE CURSE OF THE BRONZE
    LAMP $3.50
☐ Douglass, Donald M./MANY BRAVE HEARTS
    $3.50
☐ Douglass, Donald M./REBECCA'S PRIDE $3.50
☐ Fennelly, Tony/THE GLORY HOLE MURDERS
    Cloth $14.95
☐ Hughes, Dorothy/IN A LONELY PLACE $3.50
☐ Innes, Hammond/ATLANTIC FURY $3.50
☐ Innes, Hammond/THE LAND GOD GAVE TO
    CAIN $3.50
☐ Innes, Hammond/SOLOMON'S SEAL $3.50

- [ ] Innes, Hammond/THE WRECK OF THE MARY DEARE $3.50
- [ ] L'Amour, Louis/THE HILLS OF HOMOCIDE $2.95
- [ ] Lewis, Norman/THE MAN IN THE MIDDLE $3.50
- [ ] MacDonald, John D./TWO $2.50
- [ ] MacDonald, Philip/THE RASP $3.50
- [ ] Mason, A.E.W./AT THE VILLA ROSE $3.50
- [ ] Mason, A.E.W./THE HOUSE IN LORDSHIP LANE $3.50
- [ ] Mason, A.E.W./THE HOUSE OF THE ARROW $3.50
- [ ] Mason, A.E.W./THEY WOULDN'T BE CHESSMEN $3.50
- [ ] Miller, Geoffrey/THE BLACK GLOVE $3.50
- [ ] Pikser, Jeremy/JUNK ON THE HILL Cloth $13.95
- [ ] Rinehart, Mary Rogers/THE CIRCULAR STAIRCASE $3.50
- [ ] Rogers, Joel T./THE RED RIGHT HAND $3.50
- [ ] Royce, Kenneth/CHANNEL ASSAULT $3.50
- [ ] Royce, Kenneth/10,000 DAYS $3.50
- [ ] Royce, Kenneth/THE THIRD ARM $3.50
- [ ] Siodmak, Curt/DONOVAN'S BRAIN $3.50
- [ ] Woolrich, Cornell/BLIND DATE WITH DEATH $3.50
- [ ] Woolrich, Cornell/VAMPIRE'S HONEYMOON $3.50

Available at fine bookstores everywhere or use this coupon for ordering:

Carroll & Graf Publishers, Inc., 260 Fifth Avenue, N.Y., N.Y. 10001

Please send me the books I have checked above. I am enclosing $_____ (please add $1.75 per title to cover postage and handling.) Send check or money order—no cash or C.O.D.'s please. N.Y residents please add 8¼% sales tax.

Mr/Mrs/Miss _____

Address _____

City _____ State/Zip _____
Please allow four to six weeks for delivery.

FINE WORKS OF FICTION AND NON-FICTION AVAILABLE FROM CARROLL & GRAF

☐ Brown, Harry/A WALK IN THE SUN $3.95
☐ De Quincey, Thomas/CONFESSIONS OF AN ENGLISH OPIUM EATER AND OTHER WRITINGS $4.95
☐ Farrell, J.G./THE SIEGE OF KRISHNAPUR $4.95
☐ Higgins, George V./A CHOICE OF ENEMIES $3.50
☐ Hilton, James/RANDOM HARVEST $4.50
☐ Huxley, Aldous/GREY EMINENCE $4.95
☐ Innes, Hammond/THE WRECK OF THE MARY DEARE $3.50
☐ Johnson, Josephine/NOW IN NOVEMBER $4.50
☐ O'Hara, John/FROM THE TERRACE $4.95
☐ Proffitt, Nicholas/GARDENS OF STONE $3.95
☐ Purdy, James/CABOT WRIGHT BEGINS $4.50
☐ Rechy, John/BODIES AND SOULS $4.50
☐ Scott, Paul/THE LOVE PAVILION $4.50
☐ Wharton, William/SCUMBLER $3.95

Available at fine bookstores everywhere or use this coupon for ordering:

Carroll & Graf Publishers, Inc., 260 Fifth Avenue, N.Y., N.Y. 10001

Please send me the books I have checked above. I am enclosing $_____ (please add $1.75 per title to cover postage and handling.) Send check or money order— no cash or C.O.D.'s please. N.Y residents please add 8¼% sales tax.

Mr/Mrs/Miss _____

Address _____

City _____ State/Zip _____

Please allow four to six weeks for delivery.

FINE SCIENCE FICTION AND FANTASY TITLES AVAILABLE FROM CARROLL & GRAF

☐ Hodgson, William H./THE HOUSE ON THE
   BORDERLAND $3.50
☐ Mundy, Talbot/KING-OF THE KHYBER RIFLES
                                              $3.95
☐ Mundy, Talbot/OM, THE SECRET OF AHBOR
   VALLEY $3.95
☐ Stevens, Francis/CITADEL OF FEAR $3.50
☐ Stevens, Francis/CLAIMED $3.50
☐ Stevens, Francis/THE HEADS OF CERBERUS $3.50